THE CREATURE FROM CLEVELAND DEPTHS

AND OTHER TALES

THE CREATURE FROM CLEVELAND DEPTHS

AND OTHER TALES

FRITZ LEIBER

WILDSIDE PRESS

THE CREATURE FROM CLEVELAND DEPTHS
AND OTHER TALES

Published in 2007 by Wildside Press.
www.wildsidepress.com

"The Creature from Cleveland Depths" originally appeared in *Galaxy*, December, 1962. "Bread Overhead" originally appeared in *Galaxy*, February 1958. "No Great Magic" originally appeared in *Galaxy Science Fiction*, December 1963.

CONTENTS

THE CREATURE FROM CLEVELAND DEPTHS

I

"Come on, Gussy," Fay prodded quietly, "quit stalking around like a neurotic bear and suggest something for my invention team to work on. I enjoy visiting you and Daisy, but I can't stay aboveground all night."

"If being outside the shelters makes you nervous, don't come around any more," Gusterson told him, continuing to stalk. "Why doesn't your invention team think of something to invent? Why don't you? Hah!" In the "Hah!" lay triumphant condemnation of a whole way of life.

"We do," Fay responded imperturbably, "but a fresh viewpoint sometimes helps."

"I'll say it does! Fay, you burglar, I'll bet you've got twenty people like myself you milk for free ideas. First you irritate their bark and then you make the rounds every so often to draw off the latex or the maple gloop."

Fay smiled. "It ought to please you that society still has a use for you outre inner-directed types. It takes something to make a junior executive stay aboveground after dark, when the missiles are on the prowl."

"Society can't have much use for us or it'd pay us something," Gusterson sourly asserted, staring blankly at the tankless TV and kicking it lightly as he passed on.

"No, you're wrong about that, Gussy. Money's not the key goad with you inner-directeds. I got that straight from our Motivations chief."

"Did he tell you what we should use instead to pay the grocer? A deep inner sense of achievement, maybe? Fay, why should I do any free thinking for Micro Systems?"

"I'll tell you why, Gussy. Simply because you get a kick out of insulting us with sardonic ideas. If we take one of them seriously, you think we're degrading ourselves, and that pleases you even more. Like making someone laugh at a lousy pun."

Gusterson held still in his roaming and grinned. "That the reason, huh? I suppose my suggestions would have to be something in the line of ultra-subminiaturized computers, where one sinister fine-etched molecule does the work of three big bumbling brain cells?"

"Not necessarily. Micro Systems is branching out. Wheel as free as a rogue star. But I'll pass along to Promotion your one molecule-three brain cell sparkler. It's a slight exaggeration, but it's catchy."

"I'll have my kids watch your ads to see if you use it and then I'll sue the whole underworld." Gusterson frowned as he resumed his stalking. He stared puzzledly at the antique TV. "How about inventing a plutonium termite?" he said suddenly. "It would get rid of those stockpiles that are worrying you moles to death."

Fay grimaced noncommittally and cocked his head.

"Well, then, how about a beauty mask? How about that, hey? I don't mean one to repair a woman's complexion, but one she'd wear all the time that'd make her look like a 17-year-old sexpot. That'd end *her* worries."

"Hey, that's for me," Daisy called from the kitchen. "I'll make Gusterson suffer. I'll make him crawl around on his hands and knees begging my immature favors."

"No, you won't," Gusterson called back. "You having a face like that would scare the kids. Better cancel that one, Fay. Half the adult race looking like Vina Vidarsson is too awful a thought."

"Yah, you're just scared of making a million dollars," Daisy jeered.

"I sure am," Gusterson said solemnly, scanning the fuzzy floor from one murky glass wall to the other, hesitating at the TV. "How about something homey now, like a flock of little prickly cylinders that roll around the floor collecting lint and flub? They'd work by electricity, or at a pinch cats could bat 'em around. Every so often they'd be automatically herded together and the lint cleaned off the bristles."

"No good," Fay said. "There's no lint underground and cats are *verboten*. And the aboveground market doesn't amount to more moneywise than the state of Southern Illinois. Keep it grander, Gussy, and more impractical — you can't sell people merely useful ideas." From his hassock in the center of the room he looked uneasily around. "Say, did that violet tone in the glass come from the high Cleveland hydrogen bomb or is it just age and ultraviolet, like desert glass?"

"NO, somebody's grandfather liked it that color," Gusterson informed him with happy bitterness. "I like it too — the glass, I mean, not the tint. People who live in glass houses can see the stars — especially when there's a window-washing streak in their germ-plasm."

"Gussy, why don't you move underground?" Fay asked, his voice taking on a missionary note. "It's a lot easier living in one room, believe me. You don't have to tramp from room to room hunting things."

"I like the exercise," Gusterson said stoutly.

"But I bet Daisy'd prefer it underground. And your kids wouldn't have to explain why their father lives like a Red Indian. Not to mention the safety factor and insurance savings and a crypt church within easy slidewalk distance. Incidentally, we see the stars all the time, better than you do — by repeater."

"Stars by repeater," Gusterson murmured to the ceiling, pausing for God to comment. Then, "No, Fay, even if I could afford it — and stand it — I'm such a bad-luck Harry that just when I got us all safely stowed at the N minus 1 sublevel, the Soviets would discover an earthquake bomb that struck from below, and I'd have to follow everybody back to the treetops. *Hey! How about bubble homes in orbit around earth?* Micro Systems could subdivide the world's most spacious suburb and all you moles could go ellipsing. Space is as safe as there is: no air, no shock waves. Free fall's the ultimate in restfulness — great health benefits. Commute by rocket — or better yet stay home and do all your business by TV-telephone, or by waldo if it were that sort of thing. Even pet your girl by remote control — she in her bubble, you in yours, whizzing through vacuum. Oh, damn-damn-*damn-damn*-DAMN!"

He was glaring at the blank screen of the TV, his big hands clenching and unclenching.

"Don't let Fay give you apoplexy — he's not worth it," Daisy said, sticking her trim head in from the kitchen, while Fay inquired anxiously, "Gussy, what's the matter?"

"Nothing, you worm!" Gusterson roared, "Except that an hour ago I forgot to tune in on the only TV program I've wanted to hear this year — *Finnegans Wake* scored for English, Gaelic and brogue. Oh, damn-*damn*-DAMN!"

"Too bad," Fay said lightly. "I didn't know they were releasing it on flat TV too."

"Well, they were! Some things are too damn big to keep completely underground. And I had to forget! I'm always doing it — I miss everything! Look here, you rat," he blatted suddenly at Fay, shaking his finger under the latter's chin, "I'll tell you what you can have that ignorant team of yours invent. They can fix me up a mechanical secretary that I can feed orders into and that'll remind me when the exact moment comes to listen to TV or phone somebody or mail in a story or write a letter or pick up a magazine or look at an eclipse or a new orbiting station or fetch the kids from school or buy Daisy a bunch of flowers or whatever it is. It's got to be something that's always with me, not something I have to go and consult or that I can get sick of and put down somewhere. And it's got to remind me forcibly enough so that I take notice and don't just shrug it aside, like I sometimes do even when Daisy reminds me of things. That's what your stupid team can invent for me! If they do a good job, I'll pay 'em as much as fifty dollars!"

"That doesn't sound like anything so very original to me,"

Fay commented coolly, leaning back from the wagging finger. "I think all senior executives have something of that sort. At least, their secretary keeps some kind of file. . . ."

"I'm not looking for something with spiked falsies and nylons up to the neck," interjected Gusterson, whose ideas about secretaries were a trifle lurid. "I just want a mech reminder — that's all!"

"Well, I'll keep the idea in mind," Fay assured him, "along with the bubble homes and beauty masks. If we ever develop anything along those lines, I'll let you know. If it's a beauty mask, I'll bring Daisy a pilot model — to use to scare strange kids." He put his watch to his ear. "Good lord, I'm going to have to cut to make it underground before the main doors close. Just ten minutes to Second Curfew! 'Bye, Gus. 'Bye, Daze."

Two minutes later, living room lights out, they watched Fay's foreshortened antlike figure scurrying across the balding ill-lit park toward the nearest escalator.

Gusterson said, "Weird to think of that big bright space-poor glamor basement stretching around everywhere underneath. Did you remind Smitty to put a new bulb in the elevator?"

"The Smiths moved out this morning," Daisy said tonelessly. "They went underneath."

"Like cockroaches," Gusterson said. "Cockroaches leavin' a sinkin' apartment building. Next the ghosts'll be retreatin' to the shelters."

"Anyhow, from now on we're our own janitors," Daisy said.

He nodded. "Just leaves three families besides us loyal to this glass death trap. Not countin' ghosts." He sighed. Then, "You like to move below, Daisy?" he asked softly, putting his arm lightly across her shoulders. "Get a woozy eyeful of the bright lights and all for a change? Be a rat for a while? Maybe we're getting too old to be bats. I could scrounge me a company job and have a thinking closet all to myself and two secretaries with stainless steel breasts. Life'd be easier for you and a lot cleaner. And you'd sleep safer."

"That's true," she answered and paused. She ran her fingertip slowly across the murky glass, its violet tint barely perceptible against a cold dim light across the park. "But somehow," she said, snaking her arm around his waist, "I don't think I'd sleep happier — or one bit excited."

II

Three weeks later Fay, dropping in again, handed to Daisy the larger of the two rather small packages he was carrying.

"It's a so-called beauty mask," he told her, "complete with wig, eyelashes, and wettable velvet lips. It even breathes — pinholed elastiskin with a static adherence-charge. But Micro Systems had nothing to do with it, thank God. Beauty Trix put it on the market ten days ago and it's already started a teen-age craze. Some boys are wearing them too, and the police are yipping at Trix for encouraging transvestism with psychic repercussions."

"Didn't I hear somewhere that Trix is a secret subsidiary of Micro?" Gusterson demanded, rearing up from his ancient electric typewriter. "No, you're not stopping me writing, Fay — it's the gut of evening. If I do any more I won't have any juice to start with tomorrow. I got another of my insanity thrillers moving. A real id-teaser. In this one not only all the characters are crazy but the robot psychiatrist too."

"The vending machines are jumping with insanity novels," Fay commented. "Odd they're so popular."

Gusterson chortled. "The only way you outer-directed moles will accept individuality any more even in a fictional character, without your superegos getting seasick, is for them to be crazy. Hey, Daisy! Lemme see that beauty mask!"

But his wife, backing out of the room, hugged the package to her bosom and solemnly shook her head.

"A hell of a thing," Gusterson complained, "not even to be

able to see what my stolen ideas look like."

"I got a present for you too," Fay said. "Something you might think of as a royalty on all the inventions someone thought of a little ahead of you. Fifty dollars by your own evaluation." He held out the smaller package. "Your tickler."

"My *what?*" Gusterson demanded suspiciously.

"Your tickler. The mech reminder you wanted. It turns out that the file a secretary keeps to remind her boss to do certain things at certain times is called a tickler file. So we named this a tickler. Here."

Gusterson still didn't touch the package. "You mean you actually put your invention team to work on that nonsense?"

"Well, what do you think? Don't be scared of it. Here, I'll show you."

As he unwrapped the package, Fay said, "It hasn't been decided yet whether we'll manufacture it commercially. If we do, I'll put through a voucher for you — for 'development consultation' or something like that. Sorry no royalty's possible. Davidson's squad had started to work up the identical idea three years ago, but it got shelved. I found it on a snoop through the closets. There! Looks rich, doesn't it?"

On the scarred black tabletop was a dully gleaming silvery object about the size and shape of a cupped hand with fingers merging. A tiny pellet on a short near-invisible wire led off from it. On the back was a punctured area suggesting the face of a microphone; there was also a window with a date and time in hours and minutes showing through and next to that four little buttons in a row. The concave underside of the silvery "hand" was smooth except for a central area where what looked like two little rollers came through.

"It goes on your shoulder under your shirt," Fay explained, "and you tuck the pellet in your ear. We might work up bone conduction on a commercial model. Inside is an ultra-slow fine-wire recorder holding a spool that runs for a week. The clock lets you go to any place on the 7-day wire and record a message. The buttons give you variable speed in going there, so you don't waste too much time making a setting. There's a knack in fingering them efficiently, but it's easily acquired."

Fay picked up the tickler. "For instance, suppose there's a TV show you want to catch tomorrow night at twenty-two hundred." He touched the buttons. There was the faintest whirring. The clock face blurred briefly three times before showing the setting he'd mentioned. Then Fay spoke into the punctured area: "Turn on TV Channel Two, you big dummy!" He grinned over at Gusterson. "When you've got all your instructions to yourself loaded in, you synchronize with the present moment and let her roll. Fit it on your shoulder and forget it. Oh, yes, and it literally does tickle you every time it delivers an instruction. That's what the little rollers are for. Believe me, you can't ignore it. Come on, Gussy, take off your shirt and try it out. We'll feed in some instructions for the next ten minutes so you get the feel of how it works."

"I don't want to," Gusterson said. "Not right now. I want to sniff around it first. My God, it's small! Besides everything else it does, does it think?"

"Don't pretend to be an idiot, Gussy! You know very well that even with ultra-sub-micro nothing quite this small can possibly have enough elements to do any thinking."

Gusterson shrugged. "I don't know about that. I think bugs think."

Fay groaned faintly. "Bugs operate by instinct, Gussy," he said. "A patterned routine. They do not scan situations and consequences and then make decisions."

"I don't expect bugs to make decisions," Gusterson said. "For that matter I don't like people who go around alla time making decisions."

"Well, you can take it from me, Gussy, that this tickler is just a miniaturized wire recorder and clock . . . and a tickler. It doesn't do anything else."

"Not yet, maybe," Gusterson said darkly. "Not this model. Fay, I'm serious about bugs thinking. Or if they don't exactly think, they feel. They've got an interior drama. An inner glow. They're conscious. For that matter, Fay, I think all your really complex electronic computers are conscious too."

"Quit kidding, Gussy."

"Who's kidding?"

"You are. Computers simply aren't alive."

"What's alive? A word. I think computers are conscious, at least while they're operating. They've got that inner glow of awareness. They sort of . . . well . . . meditate."

"Gussy, computers haven't got any circuits for meditating. They're not programmed for mystical lucubrations. They've just got circuits for solving the problems they're on."

"Okay, you admit they've got problem-solving circuits — like a man has. I say if they've got the equipment for being conscious, they're conscious. What has wings, flies."

"Including stuffed owls and gilt eagles and dodoes — and wood-burning airplanes?"

"Maybe, under some circumstances. There *was* a wood-burning airplane. Fay," Gusterson continued, wagging his wrists for emphasis, "I really think computers are conscious. They just don't have any way of telling us that they are. Or maybe they don't have any *reason* to tell us, like the little Scotch boy who didn't say a word until he was fifteen and was supposed to be deaf and dumb."

"Why didn't he say a word?"

"Because he'd never had anything to say. Or take those Hindu fakirs, Fay, who sit still and don't say a word for thirty years or until their fingernails grow to the next village. If Hindu fakirs can do that, computers can!"

Looking as if he were masticating a lemon, Fay asked quietly, "Gussy, did you say you're working on an insanity novel?"

Gusterson frowned fiercely. "Now you're kidding," he accused Fay. "The dirty kind of kidding, too."

"I'm sorry," Fay said with light contrition. "Well, now you've sniffed at it, how about trying on Tickler?" He picked up the gleaming blunted crescent and jogged it temptingly under Gusterson's chin.

"Why should I?" Gusterson asked, stepping back. "Fay, I'm up to my ears writing a book. The last thing I want is something interrupting me to make me listen to a lot of junk and do a lot of useless things."

"But, dammit, Gussy! It was all your idea in the first place!" Fay blatted. Then, catching himself, he added, "I mean, you were one of the first people to think of this particular sort of instrument."

"Maybe so, but I've done some more thinking since then." Gusterson's voice grew a trifle solemn. "Inner-directed worthwhile thinkin'. Fay, when a man forgets to do something, it's because he really doesn't want to do it or because he's all roiled up down in his unconscious. He ought to take it as a danger signal and investigate the roiling, not hire himself a human or mech reminder."

"Bushwa," Fay retorted. "In that case you shouldn't write memorandums or even take notes."

"Maybe I shouldn't," Gusterson agreed lamely. "I'd have to think that over too."

"Ha!" Fay jeered. "No, I'll tell you what your trouble is, Gussy. You're simply scared of this contraption. You've loaded your skull with horror-story nonsense about machines sprouting minds and taking over the world — until you're even scared of a simple miniaturized and clocked recorder." He thrust it out.

"Maybe I am," Gusterson admitted, controlling a flinch. "Honestly, Fay, that thing's got a gleam in its eye as if it had ideas of its own. Nasty ideas."

"Gussy, you nut, it hasn't *got* an eye."

"Not now, no, but it's got the gleam — the eye may come. It's the Cheshire cat in reverse. If you'd step over here and look at yourself holding it, you could see what I mean. But I don't think computers *sprout* minds, Fay. I just think they've *got* minds, because they've got the mind elements."

"Ho, ho!" Fay mocked. "Everything that has a material side has a mental side," he chanted. "Everything that's a body is also a spirit. Gussy, that dubious old metaphysical dualism went out centuries ago."

"Maybe so," Gusterson said, "but we still haven't anything but that dubious dualism to explain the human mind, have we? It's a jelly of nerve cells and it's a vision of the cosmos. If that isn't dualism, what is?"

"I give up. Gussy, are you going to try out this tickler?"

"No!"

"But dammit, Gussy, we made it just for you! — practically."

"Sorry, but I'm not coming near the thing."

"Zen come near me," a husky voice intoned behind them. "Tonight I vant a man."

Standing in the door was something slim in a short silver sheath. It had golden bangs and the haughtiest snub-nosed face in the world. It slunk toward them.

"My God, Vina Vidarsson!" Gusterson yelled.

"Daisy, that's terrific," Fay applauded, going up to her.

She bumped him aside with a swing of her hips, continuing to advance. "Not you, Ratty," she said throatily. "I vant a real man."

"Fay, I suggested Vina Vidarsson's face for the beauty mask," Gusterson said, walking around his wife and shaking a finger. "Don't tell me Trix just happened to think of that too."

"What else could they think of?" Fay laughed. "This season sex means VV and nobody else." An odd little grin flicked his lips, a tic traveled up his face and his body twitched slightly. "Say, folks, I'm going to have to be leaving. It's exactly fifteen minutes to Second Curfew. Last time I had to run and I got heartburn. When *are* you people going to move downstairs? I'll leave Tickler, Gussy. Play around with it and get used to it. 'Bye now."

"Hey, Fay," Gusterson called curiously, "have you developed absolute time sense?"

Fay grinned a big grin from the doorway — almost too big a grin for so small a man. "I didn't need to," he said softly, patting his right shoulder. "My tickler told me."

He closed the door behind him.

As side-by-side they watched him strut sedately across the murky chilly-looking park, Gusterson mused, "So the little devil had one of those nonsense-gadgets on all the time and I never noticed. Can you beat that?" Something drew across the violet-tinged stars a short bright line that quickly faded. "What's that?" Gusterson asked gloomily. "Next to last stage of missile-here?"

"Won't you settle for an old-fashioned shooting star?" Daisy asked softly. The (wettable) velvet lips of the mask made even her natural voice sound different. She reached a hand back of her neck to pull the thing off.

"Hey, don't do that," Gusterson protested in a hurt voice. "Not for a while anyway."

"Hokay!" she said harshly, turning on him. "Zen down on your knees, dog!"

III

It was a fortnight and Gusterson was loping down the home stretch on his 40,000-word insanity novel before Fay dropped in again, this time promptly at high noon.

Normally Fay cringed his shoulders a trifle and was inclined to slither, but now he strode aggressively, his legs scissoring in a fast, low goosestep. He whipped off the sunglasses that all moles wore topside by day and began to pound Gusterson on the back while calling boisterously, "How are you, Gussy Old Boy, Old Boy?"

Daisy came in from the kitchen to see why Gusterson was choking. She was instantly grabbed and violently bussed to the accompaniment of, "Hiya, Gorgeous! Yum-yum! How about ad-libbing that some weekend?"

She stared at Fay dazedly, rasping the back of her hand across her mouth, while Gusterson yelled, "Quit that! What's got into you, Fay? Have they transferred you out of R & D to Company Morale? Do they line up all the secretaries at roll call and make you give them an eight-hour energizing kiss?"

"Ha, wouldn't you like to know?" Fay retorted. He grinned, twitched jumpingly, held still a moment, then hustled over to the far wall. "Look out there," he rapped, pointing through the violet glass at a gap between the two nearest old skyscraper apartments. "In thirty seconds you'll see them test the new needle bomb at the other end of Lake Erie. It's educational." He began to count off seconds, vigorously semaphoring his arm. ". . . Two . . . three . . . Gussy, I've put through a voucher for two yards for you. Budgeting squawked, but I pressured 'em."

Daisy squealed, "Yards! — are those dollar thousands?" while Gusterson was asking, "Then you're marketing the tickler?"

"Yes. Yes," Fay replied to them in turn. ". . . Nine . . . ten . . ." Again he grinned and twitched. "Time for noon Com-staff," he announced staccato. "Pardon the hush box." He whipped a pancake phone from under his coat, clapped it over his face and spoke fiercely but inaudibly into it, continuing to semaphore. Suddenly he thrust the phone away. "Twenty-nine . . . thirty . . . Thar she blows!"

An incandescent streak shot up the sky from a little above the far horizon and a doubly dazzling point of light appeared just above the top of it, with the effect of God dotting an "i".

"Ha, that'll skewer espionage satellites like swatting flies!" Fay proclaimed as the portent faded. "Bracing! Gussy, where's your tickler? I've got a new spool for it that'll razzle-dazzle you."

"I'll bet," Gusterson said drily. "Daisy?"

"You gave it to the kids and they got to fooling with it and broke it."

"No matter," Fay told them with a large sidewise sweep of

his hand. "Better you wait for the new model. It's a six-way improvement."

"So I gather," Gusterson said, eyeing him speculatively. "Does it automatically inject you with cocaine? A fix every hour on the second?"

"Ha-ha, joke. Gussy, it achieves the same effect without using any dope at all. Listen: a tickler reminds you of your duties and opportunities — your chances for happiness and success! What's the obvious next step?"

"Throw it out the window. By the way, how do you do that when you're underground?"

"We have hi-speed garbage boosts. The obvious next step is you give the tickler a heart. It not only tells you, it warmly persuades you. It doesn't just say, 'Turn on the TV Channel Two, Joyce program,' it *brills* at you, 'Kid, Old Kid, race for the TV and flip that Two Switch! There's a great show coming through the pipes this second plus ten — you'll enjoy the hell out of yourself! Grab a ticket to ecstasy!'"

"My God," Gusterson gasped, "are those the kind of jolts it's giving you now?"

"Don't you get it, Gussy? You never load your tickler except when you're feeling buoyantly enthusiastic. You don't just tell yourself what to do hour by hour next week, you sell yourself on it. That way you not only make doubly sure you'll obey instructions but you constantly reinoculate yourself with your own enthusiasm."

"I can't stand myself when I'm that enthusiastic," Gusterson said. "I feel ashamed for hours afterwards."

"You're warped — all this lonely sky-life. What's more, Gussy, think how still more persuasive some of those instructions would be if they came to a man in his best girl's most bedroomy voice, or his doctor's or psycher's if it's that sort of thing — or Vina Vidarsson's! By the way, Daze, don't wear that beauty mask outside. It's a grand misdemeanor ever since ten thousand teen-agers rioted through Tunnel-Mart wearing them. And VV's sueing Trix."

"No chance of that," Daisy said. "Gusterson got excited and bit off the nose." She pinched her own delicately.

"I'd no more obey my enthusiastic self," Gusterson was brooding, "than I'd obey a Napoleon drunk on his own brandy or a hopped-up St. Francis. Reinoculated with my own enthusiasm? I'd die just like from snake-bite!"

"Warped, I said," Fay dogmatized, stamping around. "Gussy, having the instructions persuasive instead of neutral turned out to be only the opening wedge. The next step wasn't so obvious, but I saw it. Using subliminal verbal stimuli in his tickler, a man can be given constant supportive euphoric therapy 24 hours a day! And it makes use of all that empty wire. We've revived the ideas of a pioneer dynamic psycher named Dr. Coué. For instance, right now my tickler is saying to me — in tones too soft to reach my conscious mind, but do they stab into the unconscious! — 'Day by day in every way I'm getting sharper and sharper.' It alternates that with 'gutsier and gutsier' and . . . well, forget that. Coué mostly used 'better and better' but that seems too general. And every hundredth time it says them out loud and the tickler gives me a brush — just a faint cootchto — make sure I'm keeping in touch."

"That third word-pair," Daisy wondered, feeling her mouth reminiscently. "Could I guess?"

Gusterson's eyes had been growing wider and wider. "Fay," he said, "I could no more use my mind for anything if I knew all that was going on in my inner ear than if I were being brushed down with brooms by three witches. Look here," he said with loud authority, "you got to stop all this — it's crazy. Fay, if Micro'll junk the tickler, I'll think you up something else to invent — something real good."

"Your inventing days are over," Fay brilled gleefully. "I mean, you'll never equal your masterpiece."

"How about," Gusterson bellowed, "an anti-individual guided missile? The physicists have got small-scale antigravity good enough to float and fly something the size of a hand grenade. I can smell that even though it's a back-of-the-safe military secret. Well, how about keying such a missile to a man's finger-prints — or brainwaves, maybe, or his unique smell! — so it can spot and follow him around then target in on him, without harming anyone else? Long-distance assassination — and the stinkingest gets it! Or you could simply load it with some disgusting goo and key it to teen-agers as a group — that'd take care of them. Fay, doesn't it give you a rich warm kick to think of my midget missiles buzzing around in your tunnels, seeking out evil-doers, like a swarm of angry wasps or angelic bumblebees?"

"You're not luring me down any side trails," Fay said laughingly. He grinned and twitched, then hurried toward the opposite wall, motioning them to follow. Outside, about a hundred yards beyond the purple glass, rose another ancient glass-walled apartment skyscraper. Beyond, Lake Erie rippled glintingly.

"Another bomb-test?" Gusterson asked.

Fay pointed at the building. "Tomorrow," he announced, "a modern factory, devoted solely to the manufacture of ticklers, will be erected on that site."

"You mean one of those windowless phallic eyesores?" Gusterson demanded. "Fay, you people aren't even consistent. You've got all your homes underground. Why not your factories?"

"Sh! Not enough room. And night missiles are scarier."

"I know that building's been empty for a year," Daisy said uneasily, "but how —?"

"Sh! Watch! *Now!*"

The looming building seemed to blur or fuzz for a moment. Then it was as if the lake's bright ripples had invaded the old glass a hundred yards away. Wavelets chased themselves up and down the gleaming walls, became higher, higher . . . and then suddenly the glass cracked all over to tiny fragments and fell away, to be followed quickly by fragmented concrete and plastic and plastic piping, until all that was left was the nude steel framework, vibrating so rapidly as to be almost invisible against the gleaming lake.

Daisy covered her ears, but there was no explosion, only a long-drawn-out low crash as the fragments hit twenty floors below and dust whooshed out sideways.

"Spectacular!" Fay summed up. "Knew you'd enjoy it. That little trick was first conceived by the great Tesla during his last fruity years. Research discovered it in his biog — we just made the dream come true. A tiny resonance device you could carry in your belt-bag attunes itself to the natural harmonic of a structure and then increases amplitude by tiny pushes exactly in time. Just like soldiers marching in step can break down a bridge, only this is as if it were being done by one marching ant." He pointed at the naked framework appearing out of its own blur and said, "We'll be able to hang the factory on that. If not, we'll whip a mega-current through it and vaporize it. No question the micro-resonator is the neatest sweetest wrecking device going. You can expect a lot more of this sort of efficiency now that mankind has the tickler to enable him to use his full potential. What's the matter, folks?"

Daisy was staring around the violet-walled room with dumb mistrust. Her hands were trembling.

"You don't have to worry," Fay assured her with an understanding laugh. "This building's safe for a month more at least." Suddenly he grimaced and leaped a foot in the air. He raised a clawed hand to scratch his shoulder but managed to check the movement. "Got to beat it, folks," he announced tersely. "My tickler gave me the grand cootch."

"Don't go yet," Gusterson called, rousing himself with a shudder which he immediately explained: "I just had the illusion that if I shook myself all my flesh and guts would fall off my shimmying skeleton, Brr! Fay, before you and Micro go off half cocked, I want you to know there's one insuperable objection to the tickler as a mass-market item. The average man or woman won't go to the considerable time and trouble it must take to load a tickler. He simply hasn't got the compulsive orderliness and willingness to plan that it requires."

"We thought of that weeks ago," Fay rapped, his hand on the door. "Every tickler spool that goes to market is patterned like wallpaper with one of five designs of suitable subliminal supportive euphoric material. 'Ittier and ittier,' 'viriler and viriler' — you know. The buyer is robot-interviewed for an hour, his personalized daily routine laid out and thereafter templated on his weekly spool. He's strongly urged next to take his tickler to his doctor and psycher for further instruction-imposition. We've been working with the medical profession from the start. They love the tickler because it'll remind people to take their medicine on the dot . . . and rest and eat and go to sleep just when and how doc says. This is a big operation, Gussy — a biiiiiiig operation! 'Bye!"

Daisy hurried to the wall to watch him cross the park. Deep down she was a wee bit worried that he might linger to attach a micro-resonator to *this* building and she wanted to time him. But Gusterson settled down to his typewriter and began to bat away.

"I want to have another novel started," he explained to her, "before the ant marches across this building in about four and a half weeks . . . or a million sharp little gutsy guys come swarming out of the ground and heave it into Lake Erie."

IV

Early next morning windowless walls began to crawl up the stripped skyscraper between them and the lake. Daisy pulled the black-out curtains on that side. For a day or two longer their thoughts and conversations were haunted by Gusterson's vague sardonic visions of a horde of tickler-energized moles pouring up out of the tunnels to tear down the remaining trees, tank the atmosphere and perhaps somehow dismantle the stars — at least on this side of the world — but then they both settled back into their customary easy-going routines. Gusterson typed. Daisy made her daily shopping trip to a little topside daytime store and started painting a mural on the floor of the empty apartment next theirs but one.

"We ought to lasso some neighbors," she suggested once. "I need somebody to hold my brushes and admire. How about you making a trip below at the cocktail hours, Gusterson, and picking up a couple of girls for a starter? Flash the old viriler charm, cootch them up a bit, emphasize the delights of high living, but make sure they're compatible roommates. You could pick up that two-yard check from Micro at the same time."

"You're an immoral money-ravenous wench," Gusterson said absently, trying to dream of an insanity beyond insanity that would make his next novel a real id-rousing best-vender.

"If that's your vision of me, you shouldn't have chewed up the VV mask."

"I'd really prefer you with green stripes," he told her. "But stripes, spots, or sun-bathing, you're better than those cocktail moles."

Actually both of them acutely disliked going below. They much preferred to perch in their eyrie and watch the people of Cleveland Depths, as they privately called the local sub-suburb, rush up out of the shelters at dawn to work in the concrete fields and windowless factories, make their daytime jet trips and freeway jaunts, do their noon-hour and coffee-break guerrilla practice, and then go scurrying back at twilight to the atomic-proof, brightly lit, vastly exciting, claustrophobic caves.

Fay and his projects began once more to seem dreamlike, though Gusterson did run across a cryptic advertisement for ticklers in *The Manchester Guardian*, which he got daily by facsimile. Their three children reported similar ads, of no interest to young fry, on the TV and one afternoon they came home with the startling news that the monitors at their subsurface school had been issued ticklers. On sharp interrogation by Gusterson, however, it appeared that these last were not ticklers but merely two-way radios linked to the school police station transmitter.

"Which is bad enough," Gusterson commented later to Daisy. "But it'd be even dirtier to think of those clock-watching superegos being strapped to kids' shoulders. Can you imagine Huck Finn with a tickler, tellin' him when to tie up the raft to a tow-head and when to take a swim?"

"I bet Fay could," Daisy countered. "When's he going to bring you that check, anyhow? Iago wants a jetcycle and I promised Imogene a Vina Kit and then Claudius'll have to have something."

Gusterson scowled thoughtfully. "You know, Daze," he said, "I got a feeling Fay's in the hospital, all narcotized up and being fed intravenously. The way he was jumping around last time, that tickler was going to cootch him to pieces in a week."

As if to refute this intuition, Fay turned up that very evening. The lights were dim. Something had gone wrong with the building's old transformer and, pending repairs, the two remaining occupied apartments were making do with batteries, which turned bright globes to mysterious amber candles and made Gusterson's ancient typewriter operate sluggishly.

Fay's manner was subdued or at least closely controlled and for a moment Gusterson thought he'd shed his tickler. Then the little man came out of the shadows and Gusterson saw the large bulge on his right shoulder.

"Yes, we had to up it a bit sizewise," Fay explained in clipped tones. "Additional super-features. While brilliantly successful on the whole, the subliminal euphorics were a shade too effective. Several hundred users went hoppity manic. We gentled the cootch and qualified the subliminals — you know, 'Day by day in every way I'm getting sharper *and more serene*' — but a stabilizing influence was still needed, so after a top-level conference we decided to combine Tickler with Moodmaster."

"My God," Gusterson interjected, "do they have a machine now that does that?"

"Of course. They've been using them on ex-mental patients for years."

"I just don't keep up with progress," Gusterson said, shaking his head bleakly. "I'm falling behind on all fronts."

"You ought to have your tickler remind you to read Science Service releases," Fay told him. "Or simply instruct it to scan the releases and — no, that's still in research." He looked at Gusterson's shoulder and his eyes widened. "You're not wearing the new-model tickler I sent you," he said accusingly.

"I never got it," Gusterson assured him. "Postmen deliver topside mail and parcels by throwing them on the high-speed garbage boosts and hoping a tornado will blow them to the right addresses." Then he added helpfully, "Maybe the Russians stole it while it was riding the whirlwinds."

"That's not a suitable topic for jesting," Fay frowned. "We're hoping that Tickler will mobilize the full potential of the Free World for the first time in history. Gusterson, you are going to have to wear a ticky-tick. It's becoming impossible for a man to get through modern life without one."

"Maybe I will," Gusterson said appeasingly, "but right now tell me about Moodmaster. I want to put it in my new insanity novel."

Fay shook his head. "Your readers will just think you're behind the times. If you use it, underplay it. But anyhow, Moodmaster is a simple physiotherapy engine that monitors bloodstream chemicals and body electricity. It ties directly into the bloodstream, keeping blood, sugar, et cetera, at optimum levels and injecting euphrin or depressin as necessary — and occasionally a touch of extra adrenaline, as during work emergencies."

"Is it painful?" Daisy called from the bedroom.

"Excruciating," Gusterson called back. "Excuse it,

please," he grinned at Fay. "Hey, didn't I suggest cocaine injections last time I saw you?"

"So you did," Fay agreed flatly. "Oh by the way, Gussy, here's that check for a yard I promised you. Micro doesn't muzzle the ox."

"Hooray!" Daisy cheered faintly.

"I thought you said it was going to be for two." Gusterson complained.

"Budgeting always forces a last-minute compromise," Fay shrugged. "You have to learn to accept those things."

"I love accepting money and I'm glad any time for three feet," Daisy called agreeably. "Six feet might make me wonder if I weren't an insect, but getting a yard just makes me feel like a gangster's moll."

"Want to come out and gloat over the yard paper, Toots, and stuff it in your diamond-embroidered net stocking top?" Gusterson called back.

"No, I'm doing something to that portion of me just now. But hang onto the yard, Gusterson."

"Aye-aye, Cap'n," he assured her. Then, turning back to Fay, "So you've taken the Dr. Coué repeating out of the tickler?"

"Oh, no. Just balanced it off with depressin. The subliminals are still a prime sales-point. All the tickler features are cumulative, Gussy. You're still underestimating the scope of the device."

"I guess I am. What's this 'work-emergencies' business? If you're using the tickler to inject drugs into workers to keep them going, that's really just my cocaine suggestion modernized and I'm putting in for another thou. Hundreds of years ago the South American Indians chewed coca leaves to kill fatigue sensations."

"That so? Interesting — and it proves priority for the Indians, doesn't it? I'll make a try for you, Gussy, but don't expect anything." He cleared his throat, his eyes grew distant and, turning his head a little to the right, he enunciated sharply, "Pooh-Bah. Time: Inst oh five. One oh five seven. Oh oh. Record: Gussy coca thou budget. Cut." He explained, "We got a voice-cued setter now on the deluxe models. You can record a memo to yourself without taking off your shirt. Incidentally, I use the ends of the hours for trifle-memos. I've already used up the fifty-nines and eights for tomorrow and started on the fifty-sevens."

"I understood most of your memo," Gusterson told him gruffly. "The last 'Oh oh' was for seconds, wasn't it? Now I call that crude — why not microseconds too? But how do you remember where you've made a memo so you don't rerecord over it? After all, you're rerecording over the wallpaper all the time."

"Tickler beeps and then hunts for the nearest information-free space."

"I see. And what's the Pooh-Bah for?"

Fay smiled. "Cut. My password for activating the setter, so it won't respond to chance numerals it overhears."

"But why Pooh-Bah?"

Fay grinned. "Cut. And you a writer. It's a literary reference, Gussy. Pooh-Bah (cut!) was Lord High Everything Else in *The Mikado*. He had a little list and nothing on it would ever be missed."

"Oh, yeah," Gusterson remembered, glowering. "As I recall it, all that went on that list was the names of people who were slated to have their heads chopped off by Ko-Ko. Better watch your step, Shorty. It may be a back-handed omen. Maybe all those workers you're puttin' ticklers on to pump them full of adrenaline so they'll overwork without noticin' it will revolt and come out some day choppin' for your head."

"Spare me the Marxist mythology," Fay protested. "Gussy, you've got a completely wrong slant on Tickler. It's true that most of our mass sales so far, bar government and army, have been to large companies purchasing for their employees —"

"Ah-ha!"

"— but that's because there's nothing like a tickler for

teaching a new man his job. It tells him from instant to instant what he must do — while he's already on the job and without disturbing other workers. Magnetizing a wire with a job pattern is the easiest thing going. And you'd be astonished what the subliminals do for employee morale. It's this way, Gussy: most people are too improvident and unimaginative to see in advance the advantages of ticklers. They buy one because the company strongly suggests it and payment is on easy installments withheld from salary. They find a tickler makes the work day go easier. The little fellow perched on your shoulder is a friend exuding comfort and good advice. The first thing he's set to say is 'Take it easy, pal.'

"Within a week they're wearing their tickler 24 hours a day — and buying a tickler for the wife, so she'll remember to comb her hair and smile real pretty and cook favorite dishes."

"I get it, Fay," Gusterson cut in. "The tickler is the newest fad for increasing worker efficiency. Once, I read somewheres, it was salt tablets. They had salt-tablet dispensers everywhere, even in air-conditioned offices where there wasn't a moist armpit twice a year and the gals sweat only champagne. A decade later people wondered what all those dusty white pills were for. Sometimes they were mistook for tranquilizers. It'll be the same way with ticklers. Somebody'll open a musty closet and see jumbled heaps of these gripping-hand silvery gadgets gathering dust curls and —"

"They will not!" Fay protested vehemently. "Ticklers are not a fad — they're history-changers, they're Free-World revolutionary! Why, before Micro Systems put a single one on the market, we'd made it a rule that every Micro employee had to wear one! If that's not having supreme confidence in a product —"

"Every employee except the top executives, of course," Gusterson interrupted jeeringly. "And that's not demoting you, Fay. As the R & D chief most closely involved, you'd naturally have to show special enthusiasm."

"But you're wrong there, Gussy," Fay crowed. "Man for

man, our top executives have been more enthusiastic about their personal ticklers than any other class of worker in the whole outfit."

Gusterson slumped and shook his head. "If that's the case," he said darkly, "maybe mankind deserves the tickler."

"I'll say it does!" Fay agreed loudly without thinking. Then, "Oh, can the carping, Gussy. Tickler's a great invention. Don't deprecate it just because you had something to do with its genesis. You're going to have to get in the swim and wear one."

"Maybe I'd rather drown horribly."

"Can the gloom-talk too! Gussy, I said it before and I say it again, you're just scared of this new thing. Why, you've even got the drapes pulled so you won't have to look at the tickler factory."

"Yes, I am scared," Gusterson said. "Really sca . . . AWP!"

Fay whirled around. Daisy was standing in the bedroom doorway, wearing the short silver sheath. This time there was no mask, but her bobbed hair was glitteringly silvered, while her legs, arms, hands, neck, face — every bit of her exposed skin — was painted with beautifully even vertical green stripes.

"I did it as a surprise for Gusterson," she explained to Fay. "He says he likes me this way. The green glop's supposed to be smudgeproof."

Gusterson did not comment. His face had a rapt expression. "I'll tell you why your tickler's so popular, Fay," he said softly. "It's not because it backstops the memory or because it boosts the ego with subliminals. It's because it takes the hook out of a guy, it takes over the job of withstanding the pressure of living. See, Fay, here are all these little guys in this subterranean rat race with atomic-death squares and chromium-plated reward squares and enough money if you pass Go almost to get to Go again — and a million million rules of the game to keep in mind. Well, here's this one little guy and every morning he wakes up there's all these things he's got to keep in mind to do or he'll lose his turn three times in a row and maybe a terrible black rook in iron armor'll loom up and bang him off the chessboard. But now, look, now he's got his tickler and he tells his sweet silver tickler all these things and the tickler's got to remember them. Of course he'll have to do them eventually but meanwhile the pressure's off him, the hook's out of his short hairs. He's shifted the responsibility. . . ."

"Well, what's so bad about that?" Fay broke in loudly. "What's wrong with taking the pressure off little guys? Why shouldn't Tickler be a super-ego surrogate? Micro's Motivations chief noticed that positive feature straight off and scored it three pluses. Besides, it's nothing but a gaudy way of saying that Tickler backstops the memory. Seriously, Gussy, what's so bad about it?"

"I don't know," Gusterson said slowly, his eyes still far away. "I just know it feels bad to me." He crinkled his big forehead. "Well for one thing," he said, "it means that a man's taking orders from something else. He's got a kind of master. He's sinking back into a slave psychology."

"He's only taking orders from himself," Fay countered disgustedly. "Tickler's just a mech reminder, a notebook, in essence no more than the back of an old envelope. It's no master."

"Are you absolutely sure of that?" Gusterson asked quietly.

"Why, Gussy, you big oaf —" Fay began heatedly. Suddenly his features quirked and he twitched. "'Scuse me, folks," he said rapidly, heading for the door, "but my tickler told me I gotta go."

"Hey Fay, don't you mean you told your tickler to tell you when it was time to go?" Gusterson called after him.

Fay looked back in the doorway. He wet his lips, his eyes moved from side to side. "I'm not quite sure," he said in an odd strained voice and darted out.

Gusterson stared for some seconds at the pattern of emptiness Fay had left. Then he shivered. Then he shrugged. "I must be slipping," he muttered. "I never even suggested something for him to invent." Then he looked around at Daisy, who was still standing poker-faced in her doorway.

"Hey, you look like something out of the Arabian Nights," he told her. "Are you supposed to be anything special? How far do those stripes go, anyway?"

"You could probably find out," she told him coolly. "All you have to do is kill me a dragon or two first."

He studied her. "My God," he said reverently, "I really have all the fun in life. What do I do to deserve this?"

"You've got a big gun," she told him, "and you go out in the world with it and hold up big companies and take yards and yards of money away from them in rolls like ribbon and bring it all home to me."

"Don't say that about the gun again," he said. "Don't whisper it, don't even think it. I've got one, dammit — thirty-eight caliber, yet — and I don't want some psionic monitor with two-way clairaudience they haven't told me about catching the whisper and coming to take the gun away from us. It's one of the few individuality symbols we've got left."

Suddenly Daisy whirled away from the door, spun three times so that her silvered hair stood out like a metal coolie hat, and sank to a curtsey in the middle of the room.

"I've just thought of what I am," she announced, fluttering her eyelashes at him. "I'm a sweet silver tickler with green stripes."

V

Next day Daisy cashed the Micro check for ten hundred silver smackers, which she hid in a broken radionic coffee urn. Gusterson sold his insanity novel and started a new one about a mad medic with a hiccupy hysterical chuckle, who gimmicked Moodmasters to turn mental patients into nymphomaniacs, mass murderers and compulsive saints. But this time he couldn't get Fay out of his mind, or the last chilling words the nervous little man had spoken.

For that matter, he couldn't blank the underground out of his mind as effectively as usually. He had the feeling that a new kind of mole was loose in the burrows and that the ground at the foot of their skyscraper might start humping up any minute.

Toward the end of one afternoon he tucked a half dozen newly typed sheets in his pocket, shrouded his typer, went to the hatrack and took down his prize: a miner's hard-top cap with electric headlamp.

"Goin' below, Cap'n," he shouted toward the kitchen.

"Be back for second dog watch," Daisy replied. "Remember what I told you about lassoing me some art-conscious girl neighbors."

"Only if I meet a piebald one with a taste for Scotch — or maybe a pearl gray biped jaguar with violet spots," Gusterson told her, clapping on the cap with a We-Who-Are-About-To-Die gesture.

Halfway across the park to the escalator bunker Gusterson's heart began to tick. He resolutely switched on his headlamp.

As he'd known it would, the hatch robot whirred an extra and higher-pitched ten seconds when it came to his topside address, but it ultimately dilated the hatch for him, first handing him a claim check for his ID card.

Gusterson's heart was ticking like a sledgehammer by now. He hopped clumsily onto the escalator, clutched the moving guard rail to either side, then shut his eyes as the steps went over the edge and became what felt like vertical. An instant later he forced his eyes open, unclipped a hand from the rail and touched the second switch beside his headlamp, which instantly began to blink whitely, as if he were a civilian plane flying into a nest of military jobs.

With a further effort he kept his eyes open and flinchingly surveyed the scene around him. After zigging through a bombproof half-furlong of roof, he was dropping into a large twilit cave. The blue-black ceiling twinkled with stars. The walls were pierced at floor level by a dozen archways with busy niche stores and glowing advertisements crowded between them. From the archways some three dozen slidewalks curved out, tangenting off each other in a bewildering multiple cloverleaf. The slidewalks were packed with people, traveling motionless like purposeful statues or pivoting with practiced grace from one slidewalk to another, like a thousand toreros doing veronicas.

The slidewalks were moving faster than he recalled from his last venture underground and at the same time the whole pedestrian concourse was quieter than he remembered. It was as if the five thousand or so moles in view were all listening — for what? But there was something else that had changed about them — a change that he couldn't for a moment define, or unconsciously didn't want to. Clothing style? No . . . My God, they weren't all wearing identical monster masks? No . . . Hair color? . . . Well. . . .

He was studying them so intently that he forgot his escalator was landing. He came off it with a heel-jarring stumble and bumped into a knot of four men on the tiny triangular hold-still. These four at least sported a new style-wrinkle: ribbed gray shoulder-capes that made them look as if their heads were poking up out of the center of bulgy umbrellas or giant mushrooms.

One of them grabbed hold of Gusterson and saved him from staggering onto a slidewalk that might have carried him to Toledo.

"Gussy, you dog, you must have esped I wanted to see you," Fay cried, patting him on the elbows. "Meet Davidson and Kester and Hazen, colleagues of mine. We're all Micromen." Fay's companions were staring strangely at Gusterson's blinking headlamp. Fay explained rapidly, "Mr. Gusterson is an insanity novelist. You know, I-D."

"Inner-directed spells *id*," Gusterson said absently, still staring at the interweaving crowd beyond them, trying to figure out what made them different from last trip. "Creativity fuel. Cranky. Explodes through the parietal fissure if you look at it cross-eyed."

"Ha-ha," Fay laughed. "Well, boys, I've found my man. How's the new novel perking, Gussy?"

"Got my climax, I think," Gusterson mumbled, still peering puzzledly around Fay at the slidestanders. "Moodmaster's going to come alive. Ever occur to you that 'mood' is 'doom' spelled backwards? And then. . . ." He let his voice trail off as he realized that Kester and Davidson and Hazen had made their farewells and were sliding into the distance. He reminded himself wryly that nobody ever wants to hear an author talk — he's much too good a listener to be wasted that way. Let's see, was it that everybody in the crowd had the same facial expression. . . ? Or showed symptoms of the same disease. . . ?

"I was coming to visit you, but now you can pay me a call," Fay was saying. "There are two matters I want to —"

Gusterson stiffened. "My God, *they're all hunchbacked!*" he yelled.

"Shh! Of course they are," Fay whispered reprovingly. "They're all wearing their ticklers. But you don't need to be insulting about it."

"*I'm gettin' out o' here.*" Gusterson turned to flee as if from five thousand Richard the Thirds.

"Oh no you're not," Fay amended, drawing him back with one hand. Somehow, underground, the little man seemed to carry more weight. "You're having cocktails in my thinking box. Besides, climbing a down escaladder will give you a heart attack."

In his home habitat, Gusterson was about as easy to handle as a rogue rhinoceros, but away from it — and especially if underground — he became more like a pliable elephant. All his bones dropped out through his feet, as he described it to

Daisy. So now he submitted miserably as Fay surveyed him up and down, switched off his blinking headlamp ("That coal-miner caper is corny, Gussy.") and then — surprisingly — rapidly stuffed his belt-bag under the right shoulder of Gusterson's coat and buttoned the latter to hold it in place.

"So you won't stand out," he explained. Another swift survey. "You'll do. Come on, Gussy. I got lots to brief you on." Three rapid paces and then Gusterson's feet would have gone out from under him except that Fay gave him a mighty shove. The small man sprang onto the slidewalk after him and then they were skimming effortlessly side by side.

Gusterson felt frightened and twice as hunchbacked as the slidestanders around him — morally as well as physically.

Nevertheless he countered bravely, "I got things to brief *you* on. I got six pages of cautions on ti —"

"Shh!" Fay stopped him. "Let's use my hushbox."

He drew out his pancake phone and stretched it so that it covered both their lower faces, like a double yashmak. Gusterson, his neck pushing into the ribbed bulge of the shoulder cape so he could be cheek to cheek with Fay, felt horribly conspicuous, but then he noticed that none of the slidestanders were paying them the least attention. The reason for their abstraction occurred to him. They were listening to their ticklers! He shuddered.

"I got six pages of caution on ticklers," he repeated into the hot, moist quiet of the pancake phone. "I typed 'em so I wouldn't forget 'em in the heat of polemicking. I want you to read every word. Fay, I've had it on my mind ever since I started wondering whether it was you or your tickler made you duck out of our place last time you were there. I want you to —"

"Ha-ha! All in good time." In the pancake phone Fay's laugh was brassy. "But I'm glad you've decided to lend a hand, Gussy. This thing is moving faaaasst. Nationwise, adult underground ticklerization is 90 per cent complete."

"I don't believe that," Gusterson protested while glaring

at the hunchbacks around them. The slidewalk was gliding down a low glow-ceiling tunnel lined with doors and advertisements. Rapt-eyed people were pirouetting on and off. "A thing just can't develop that fast, Fay. It's against nature."

"Ha, but we're not in nature, we're in culture. The progress of an industrial scientific culture is geometric. It goes n-times as many jumps as it takes. More than geometric — exponential. Confidentially, Micro's Math chief tells me we're currently on a fourth-power progress curve trending into a fifth."

"You mean we're goin' so fast we got to watch out we don't bump ourselves in the rear when we come around again?" Gusterson asked, scanning the tunnel ahead for curves. "Or just shoot straight up to infinity?"

"Exactly! Of course most of the last power and a half is due to Tickler itself. Gussy, the tickler's already eliminated absenteeism, alcoholism and aboulia in numerous urban areas — and that's just one letter of the alphabet! If Tickler doesn't turn us into a nation of photo-memory constant-creative-flow geniuses in six months, I'll come live topside."

"You mean because a lot of people are standing around glassy-eyed listening to something mumbling in their ear that it's a good thing?"

"Gussy, you don't know progress when you see it. Tickler is the greatest invention since language. Bar none, it's the greatest instrument ever devised for integrating a man into all phases of his environment. Under the present routine a newly purchased tickler first goes to government and civilian defense for primary patterning, then to the purchaser's employer, then to his doctor-psycher, then to his local bunker captain, then to *him*. *Everything* that's needful for a man's welfare gets on the spools. Efficiency cubed! Incidentally, Russia's got the tickler now. Our dip-satellites have photographed it. It's like ours except the Commies wear it on the left shoulder . . . but they're two weeks behind us developmentwise and they'll never close the gap!"

Gusterson reared up out of the pancake phone to take a deep breath. A sulky-lipped sylph-figured girl two feet from him twitched — medium cootch, he judged — then fumbled in her belt-bag for a pill and popped it in her mouth.

"Hell, the tickler's not even efficient yet about little things," Gusterson blatted, diving back into the privacy-yashmak he was sharing with Fay. "Whyn't that girl's doctor have the Moodmaster component of her tickler inject her with medicine?"

"Her doctor probably wants her to have the discipline of pill-taking — or the exercise," Fay answered glibly. "Look sharp now. Here's where we fork. I'm taking you through Micro's postern."

A ribbon of slidewalk split itself from the main band and angled off into a short alley. Gusterson hardly felt the constant-speed juncture as they crossed it. Then the secondary ribbon speeded up, carrying them at about 30 feet a second toward the blank concrete wall in which the alley ended. Gusterson prepared to jump, but Fay grabbed him with one hand and with the other held up toward the wall a badge and a button. When they were about ten feet away the wall whipped aside, then whipped shut behind them so fast that Gusterson wondered momentarily if he still had his heels and the seat of his pants.

Fay, tucking away his badge and pancake phone, dropped the button in Gusterson's vest pocket. "Use it when you leave," he said casually. "That is, if you leave."

Gusterson, who was trying to read the Do and Don't posters papering the walls they were passing, started to probe that last sinister supposition, but just then the ribbon slowed, a swinging door opened and closed behind them and they found themselves in a luxuriously furnished thinking box measuring at least eight feet by five.

"Hey, this is something," Gusterson said appreciatively to show he wasn't an utter yokel. Then, drawing on research he'd done for period novels, "Why, it's as big as a Pullman car compartment, or a first mate's cabin in the War of 1812. You really must rate."

Fay nodded, smiled wanly and sat down with a sigh on a compact overstuffed swivel chair. He let his arms dangle and his head sink into his puffed shoulder cape. Gusterson stared at him. It was the first time he could ever recall the little man showing fatigue.

"Tickler currently does have one serious drawback," Fay volunteered. "It weighs 28 pounds. You feel it when you've been on your feet a couple of hours. No question we're going to give the next model that antigravity feature you mentioned for pursuit grenades. We'd have had it in this model except there were so many other things to be incorporated." He sighed again. "Why, the scanning and decision-making elements alone tripled the mass."

"Hey," Gusterson protested, thinking especially of the sulky-lipped girl, "do you mean to tell me all those other people were toting two stone?"

Fay shook his head heavily. "They were all wearing Mark 3 or 4. I'm wearing Mark 6," he said, as one might say, "I'm carrying the genuine Cross, not one of the balsa ones."

But then his face brightened a little and he went on. "Of course the new improved features make it more than worth it . . . and you hardly feel it at all at night when you're lying down . . . and if you remember to talcum under it twice a day, no sores develop . . . at least not very big ones. . . ."

Backing away involuntarily, Gusterson felt something prod his right shoulderblade. Ripping open his coat, he convulsively plunged his hand under it and tore out Fay's belt-bag . . . and then set it down very gently on the top of a shallow cabinet and relaxed with the sigh of one who has escaped a great, if symbolic, danger. Then he remembered something Fay had mentioned. He straightened again.

"Hey, you said it's got scanning and decision-making elements. That means your tickler thinks, even by your fancy standards. And if it thinks, it's conscious."

"Gussy," Fay said wearily, frowning, "all sorts of things nowadays have S&DM elements. Mail sorters, missiles, robot medics, high-style mannequins, just to name some of the Ms. They 'think,' to use that archaic word, but it's neither here nor there. And they're certainly not conscious."

"Your tickler thinks," Gusterson repeated stubbornly, "just like I warned you it would. It sits on your shoulder, ridin' you like you was a pony or a starved St. Bernard, and now it thinks."

"Suppose it does?" Fay yawned. "What of it?" He gave a rapid sinuous one-sided shrug that made it look for a moment as if his left arm had three elbows. It stuck in Gusterson's mind, for he had never seen Fay use such a gesture and he wondered where he'd picked it up. Maybe imitating a double-jointed Micro Finance chief? Fay yawned again and said, "Please, Gussy, don't disturb me for a minute or so." His eyes half closed.

Gusterson studied Fay's sunken-cheeked face and the great puff of his shoulder cape.

"Say, Fay," he asked in a soft voice after about five minutes, "are you meditating?"

"Why, no," Fay responded, starting up and then stifling another yawn. "Just resting a bit. I seem to get more tired these days, somehow. You'll have to excuse me, Gussy. But what made you think of meditation?"

"Oh, I just got to wonderin' in that direction," Gusterson said. "You see, when you first started to develop Tickler, it occurred to me that there was one thing about it that might be real good even if you did give it S&DM elements. It's this: having a mech secretary to take charge of his obligations and routine in the real world might allow a man to slide into the other world, the world of thoughts and feelings and intuitions, and sort of ooze around in there and accomplish things. Know any of the people using Tickler that way, hey?"

"Of course not," Fay denied with a bright incredulous laugh. "Who'd want to loaf around in an imaginary world and take a chance of *missing out on what his tickler's doing?* — I mean, on what his tickler has in store for him — what he's *told* his tickler to have in store for him."

Ignoring Gusterson's shiver, Fay straightened up and seemed to brisken himself. "Ha, that little slump did me good. A tickler *makes* you rest, you know — it's one of the great things about it. Pooh-Bah's kinder to me than I ever was to myself." He buttoned open a tiny refrigerator and took out two waxed cardboard cubes and handed one to Gusterson. "Martini? Hope you don't mind drinking from the carton. Cheers. Now, Gussy old pal, there are two matters I want to take up with you —"

"Hold it," Gusterson said with something of his old authority. "There's something I got to get off my mind first." He pulled the typed pages out of his inside pocket and straightened them. "I told you about these," he said. "I want you to read them before you do anything else. Here."

Fay looked toward the pages and nodded, but did not take them yet. He lifted his hands to his throat and unhooked the clasp of his cape, then hesitated.

"You wear that thing to hide the hump your tickler makes?" Gusterson filled in. "You got better taste than those other moles."

"Not to hide it, exactly," Fay protested, "but just so the others won't be jealous. I wouldn't feel comfortable parading a free-scanning decision-capable Mark 6 tickler in front of people who can't buy it — until it goes on open sale at twenty-two fifteen tonight. Lot of shelterfolk won't be sleeping tonight. They'll be queued up to trade in their old tickler for a Mark 6 almost as good as Pooh-Bah."

He started to jerk his hands apart, hesitated again with an oddly apprehensive look at the big man, then whirled off the cape.

VI

Gusterson sucked in such a big gasp that he hiccuped. The right shoulder of Fay's jacket and shirt had been cut away. Thrusting up through the neatly hemmed hole was a silvery gray hump with a one-eyed turret atop it and two multi-jointed metal arms ending in little claws.

It looked like the top half of a pseudo-science robot — a squat evil child robot, Gusterson told himself, which had lost its legs in a railway accident — and it seemed to him that a red fleck was moving around imperceptibly in the huge single eye.

"I'll take that memo now," Fay said coolly, reaching out his hand. He caught the rustling sheets as they slipped from Gusterson's fingers, evened them up very precisely by tapping them on his knee . . . and then handed them over his shoulder to his tickler, which clicked its claws around either margin and then began rather swiftly to lift the top sheet past its single eye at a distance of about six inches.

"The first matter I want to take up with you, Gussy," Fay began, paying no attention whatsoever to the little scene on his shoulder, "— or warn you about, rather — is the imminent ticklerization of schoolchildren, geriatrics, convicts and topsiders. At three zero zero tomorrow ticklers become mandatory for all adult shelterfolk. The mop-up operations won't be long in coming — in fact, these days we find that the square root of the estimated time of a new development is generally the best time estimate. Gussy, I strongly advise you to start wearing a tickler now. And Daisy and your moppets. If you heed my advice, your kids will have the jump on your class. Transition and conditioning are easy, since Tickler itself sees to it."

Pooh-Bah leafed the first page to the back of the packet and began lifting the second past his eye — a little more swiftly than the first.

"I've got a Mark 6 tickler all warmed up for you," Fay

pressed, "*and* a shoulder cape. You won't feel one bit conspicuous." He noticed the direction of Gusterson's gaze and remarked, "Fascinating mechanism, isn't it? Of course 28 pounds are a bit oppressive, but then you have to remember it's only a way-station to free-floating Mark 7 or 8."

Pooh-Bah finished page two and began to race through page three.

"But I wanted *you* to read it," Gusterson said bemusedly, staring.

"Pooh-Bah will do a better job than I could," Fay assured him. "Get the gist without losing the chaff."

"But dammit, it's all about *him*," Gusterson said a little more strongly. "He won't be objective about it."

"A better job," Fay reiterated, "*and* more fully objective. Pooh-Bah's set for full precis. Stop worrying about it. He's a dispassionate machine, not a fallible, emotionally disturbed human misled by the will-o'-the-wisp of consciousness. Second matter: Micro Systems is impressed by your contributions to Tickler and will recruit you as a senior consultant with a salary and thinking box as big as my own, family quarters to match. It's an unheard-of high start. Gussy, I think you'd be a fool —"

He broke off, held up a hand for silence, and his eyes got a listening look. Pooh-Bah had finished page six and was holding the packet motionless. After about ten seconds Fay's face broke into a big fake smile. He stood up, suppressing a wince, and held out his hand. "Gussy," he said loudly, "I am happy to inform you that all your fears about Tickler are so much thistledown. My word on it. There's nothing to them at all. Pooh-Bah's precis, which he's just given to me, proves it."

"Look," Gusterson said solemnly, "there's one thing I want you to do. Purely to humor an old friend. But I want you to do it. *Read that memo yourself.*"

"Certainly I will, Gussy," Fay continued in the same ebullient tones. "I'll read it —" he twitched and his smile disappeared — "a little later."

"Sure," Gusterson said dully, holding his hand to his stomach. "And now if you don't mind, Fay, I'm goin' home. I feel just a bit sick. Maybe the ozone and the other additives in your shelter air are too heady for me. It's been years since I tramped through a pine forest."

"But Gussy! You've hardly got here. You haven't even sat down. Have another martini. Have a seltzer pill. Have a whiff of oxy. Have a —"

"No, Fay, I'm going home right away. I'll think about the job offer. *Remember to read that memo.*"

"I will, Gussy, I certainly will. You know your way? The button takes you through the wall. 'Bye, now."

He sat down abruptly and looked away. Gusterson pushed through the swinging door. He tensed himself for the step across onto the slowly-moving reverse ribbon. Then on a impulse he pushed ajar the swinging door and looked back inside.

Fay was sitting as he'd left him, apparently lost in listless brooding. On his shoulder Pooh-Bah was rapidly crossing and uncrossing its little metal arms, tearing the memo to smaller and smaller shreds. It let the scraps drift slowly toward the floor and oddly writhed its three-elbowed left arm . . . and then Gusterson knew from whom, or rather from what, Fay had copied his new shrug.

VII

When Gusterson got home toward the end of the second dog watch, he slipped aside from Daisy's questions and set the children laughing with a graphic enactment of his slide-standing technique and a story about getting his head caught in a thinking box built for a midget physicist. After supper he played with Imogene, Iago and Claudius until it was their bedtime and thereafter was unusually attentive to Daisy, admiring her fading green stripes, though he did spend a while in the next apartment, where they stored their outdoor camping equipment.

But the next morning he announced to the children that it was a holiday — the Feast of St. Gustersonan — d then took Daisy into the bedroom and told her everything.

When he'd finished she said, "This is something I've got to see for myself."

Gusterson shrugged. "If you think you've got to. I say we should head for the hills right now. One thing I'm standing on: the kids aren't going back to school."

"Agreed," Daisy said. "But, Gusterson, we've lived through a lot of things without leaving home altogether. We lived through the Everybody-Six-Feet-Underground-by-Christmas campaign and the Robot Watchdog craze, when you got your left foot half chewed off. We lived through the Venomous Bats and Indoctrinated Saboteur Rats and the Hypnotized Monkey Paratrooper scares. We lived through the Voice of Safety and Anti-Communist Somno-Instruction and Rightest Pills and Jet-Propelled Vigilantes. We lived through the Cold-Out, when you weren't supposed to turn on a toaster for fear its heat would be a target for prowl missiles and when people with fevers were unpopular. We lived through —"

Gusterson patted her hand. "You go below," he said. "Come back when you've decided this is different. Come back as soon as you can anyway. I'll be worried about you every minute you're down there."

When she was gone — in a green suit and hat to minimize or at least justify the effect of the faded stripes — Gusterson doled out to the children provender and equipment for a camping expedition to the next floor. Iago led them off in stealthy Indian file. Leaving the hall door open Gusterson got out his .38 and cleaned and loaded it, meanwhile concentrating on a chess problem with the idea of confusing a hypothetical psionic monitor. By the time he had hid the revolver again he heard the elevator creaking back up.

Daisy came dragging in without her hat, looking as if

she'd been concentrating on a chess problem for hours herself and just now given up. Her stripes seemed to have vanished; then Gusterson decided this was because her whole complexion was a touch green.

She sat down on the edge of the couch and said without looking at him, "Did you tell me, Gusterson, that everybody was quiet and abstracted and orderly down below, especially the ones wearing ticklers, meaning pretty much everybody?"

"I did," he said. "I take it that's no longer the case. What are the new symptoms?"

She gave no indication. After some time she said, "Gusterson, do you remember the Doré illustrations to the *Inferno*? Can you visualize the paintings of Hieronymous Bosch with the hordes of proto-Freudian devils tormenting people all over the farmyard and city square? Did you ever see the Disney animations of Moussorgsky's witches' sabbath music? Back in the foolish days before you married me, did that drug-addict girl friend of yours ever take you to a genuine orgy?"

"As bad as that, hey?"

She nodded emphatically and all of a sudden shivered violently. "Several shades worse," she said. "If they decide to come topside —" She shot up. "Where are the kids?"

"Upstairs campin' in the mysterious wilderness of the 21st floor," Gusterson reassured her. "Let's leave 'em there until we're ready to —"

He broke off. They both heard the faint sound of thudding footsteps.

"They're on the stairs," Daisy whispered, starting to move toward the open door. "But are they coming from up or down?"

"It's just one person," judged Gusterson, moving after his wife. "Too heavy for one of the kids."

The footsteps doubled in volume and came rapidly closer. Along with them there was an agonized gasping. Daisy stopped, staring fearfully at the open doorway. Gusterson moved past her. Then he stopped too.

Fay stumbled into view and would have fallen on his face except he clutched both sides of the doorway halfway up. He was stripped to the waist. There was a little blood on his shoulder. His narrow chest was arching convulsively, the ribs standing out starkly, as he sucked in oxygen to replace what he'd burned up running up twenty flights. His eyes were wild.

"They've taken over," he panted. Another gobbling breath. "Gone crazy." Two more gasps. "Gotta stop 'em."

His eyes filmed. He swayed forward. Then Gusterson's big arms were around him and he was carrying him to the couch.

Daisy came running from the kitchen with a damp cool towel. Gusterson took it from her and began to mop Fay off. He sucked in his own breath as he saw that Fay's right ear was raw and torn. He whispered to Daisy, "Look at where the thing savaged him."

The blood on Fay's shoulder came from his ear. Some of it stained a flush-skin plastic fitting that had two small valved holes in it and that puzzled Gusterson until he remembered that Moodmaster tied into the bloodstream. For a second he thought he was going to vomit.

The dazed look slid aside from Fay's eyes. He was gasping less painfully now. He sat up, pushing the towel away, buried his face in his hands for a few seconds, then looked over the fingers at the two of them.

"I've been living in a nightmare for the last week," he said in a taut small voice, "knowing the thing had come alive and trying to pretend to myself that it hadn't. Knowing it was taking charge of me more and more. Having it whisper in my ear, over and over again, in a cracked little rhyme that I could only hear every hundredth time, 'Day by day, in every way, you're learning to listen . . . and *obey*. Day by day —'"

His voice started to go high. He pulled it down and continued harshly, "I ditched it this morning when I showered. It let me break contact to do that. It must have figured it had complete control of me, mounted or dismounted. I think it's telepathic, and then it did some, well, rather unpleasant things to me late last night. But I pulled together my fears and my will and I ran for it. The slidewalks were chaos. The Mark 6 ticklers showed some purpose, though I couldn't tell you what, but as far as I could see the Mark 3s and 4s were just cootching their mounts to death — Chinese feather torture. Giggling, gasping, choking . . . gales of mirth. People are dying of laughter . . . ticklers! . . . the irony of it! It was the complete lack of order and sanity and that let me get topside. There were things I saw —" Once again his voice went shrill. He clapped his hand to his mouth and rocked back and forth on the couch.

Gusterson gently but firmly laid a hand on his good shoulder. "Steady," he said. "Here, swallow this."

Fay shoved aside the short brown drink. "We've got to stop them," he cried. "Mobilize the topsiders — contact the wilderness patrols and manned satellites — pour ether in the tunnel airpumps — invent and crash-manufacture missiles that will home on ticklers without harming humans — SOS Mars and Venus — dope the shelter water supply — do something! Gussy, you don't realize what people are going through down there every second."

"I think they're experiencing the ultimate in outer-directedness," Gusterson said gruffly.

"Have you no heart?" Fay demanded. His eyes widened, as if he were seeing Gusterson for the first time. Then, accusingly, pointing a shaking finger: "*You invented the tickler, George Gusterson! It's all your fault! You've got to do something about it!*"

Before Gusterson could retort to that, or begin to think of a reply, or even assimilate the full enormity of Fay's statement, he was grabbed from behind and frog-marched away from Fay and something that felt remarkably like the muzzle of a large-caliber gun was shoved in the small of his back.

Under cover of Fay's outburst a huge crowd of people had

entered the room from the hall — eight, to be exact. But the weirdest thing about them to Gusterson was that from the first instant he had the impression that only one mind had entered the room and that it did not reside in any of the eight persons, even though he recognized three of them, but in something that they were carrying.

Several things contributed to this impression. The eight people all had the same blank expression — watchful yet empty-eyed. They all moved in the same slithery crouch. And they had all taken off their shoes. Perhaps, Gusterson thought wildly, they believed he and Daisy ran a Japanese flat.

Gusterson was being held by two burly women, one of them quite pimply. He considered stamping on her toes, but just at that moment the gun dug in his back with a corkscrew movement.

The man holding the gun on him was Fay's colleague Davidson. Some yards beyond Fay's couch, Kester was holding a gun on Daisy, without digging it into her, while the single strange man holding Daisy herself was doing so quite decorously — a circumstance which afforded Gusterson minor relief, since it made him feel less guilty about not going berserk.

Two more strange men, one of them in purple lounging pajamas, the other in the gray uniform of a slidewalk inspector, had grabbed Fay's skinny upper arms, one on either side, and were lifting him to his feet, while Fay was struggling with such desperate futility and gibbering so pitifully that Gusterson momentarily had second thoughts about the moral imperative to go berserk when menaced by hostile force. But again the gun dug into him with a twist.

Approaching Fay face-on was the third Micro-man Gusterson had met yesterday — Hazen. It was Hazen who was carrying — quite reverently or solemnly — or at any rate very carefully the object that seemed to Gusterson to be the mind of the little storm troop presently desecrating the sanctity of his own individual home.

All of them were wearing ticklers, of course — the three

Micro-men the heavy emergent Mark 6s with their clawed and jointed arms and monocular cephalic turrets, the rest lower-numbered Marks of the sort that merely made Richard-the-Third humps under clothing.

The object that Hazen was carrying was the Mark 6 tickler Gusterson had seen Fay wearing yesterday. Gusterson was sure it was Pooh-Bah because of its air of command, and because he would have sworn on a mountain of Bibles that he recognized the red fleck lurking in the back of its single eye. And Pooh-Bah alone had the aura of full conscious thought. Pooh-Bah alone had mana.

It is not good to see an evil legless child robot with dangling straps bossing — apparently by telepathic power — not only three objects of its own kind and five close primitive relatives, but also eight human beings . . . and in addition throwing into a state of twitching terror one miserable, thin-chested, half-crazy research-and-development director.

Pooh-Bah pointed a claw at Fay. Fay's handlers dragged him forward, still resisting but more feebly now, as if half-hypnotized or at least cowed.

Gusterson grunted an outraged, "Hey!" and automatically struggled a bit, but once more the gun dug in. Daisy shut her eyes, then firmed her mouth and opened them again to look.

Seating the tickler on Fay's shoulder took a little time, because two blunt spikes in its bottom had to be fitted into the valved holes in the flush-skin plastic disk. When at last they plunged home Gusterson felt very sick indeed — and then even more so, as the tickler itself poked a tiny pellet on a fine wire into Fay's ear.

The next moment Fay had straightened up and motioned his handlers aside. He tightened the straps of his tickler around his chest and under his armpits. He held out a hand and someone gave him a shoulderless shirt and coat. He slipped into them smoothly, Pooh-Bah dexterously using its little claws to help put its turret and body through the neatly hemmed holes. The small storm troop looked at Fay with deferential expectation. He held still for a moment, as if thinking, and then walked over to Gusterson and looked him in the face and again held still.

Fay's expression was jaunty on the surface, agonized underneath. Gusterson knew that he wasn't thinking at all, but only listening for instructions from something that was whispering on the very threshold of his inner ear.

"Gussy, old boy," Fay said, twitching a depthless grin, "I'd be very much obliged if you'd answer a few simple questions." His voice was hoarse at first but he swallowed twice and corrected that. "What exactly did you have in mind when you invented ticklers? What exactly are they supposed to be?"

"Why, you miserable —" Gusterson began in a kind of confused horror, then got hold of himself and said curtly, "They were supposed to be mech reminders. They were supposed to record memoranda and —"

Fay held up a palm and shook his head and again listened for a space. Then, "That's how ticklers were supposed to be of use to humans," he said. "I don't mean that at all. I mean how ticklers were supposed to be of use to themselves. Surely you had some notion." Fay wet his lips. "If it's any help," he added, "keep in mind that it's not Fay who's asking this question, but Pooh-Bah."

Gusterson hesitated. He had the feeling that every one of the eight dual beings in the room was hanging on his answer and that something was boring into his mind and turning over his next thoughts and peering at and under them before he had a chance to scan them himself. Pooh-Bah's eye was like a red searchlight.

"Go on," Fay prompted. "What were ticklers supposed to be — for themselves?"

"Nothin'," Gusterson said softly. "Nothin' at all."

He could feel the disappointment well up in the room — and with it a touch of something like panic.

This time Fay listened for quite a long while. "I hope you

don't mean that, Gussy," he said at last very earnestly. "I mean, I hope you hunt deep and find some ideas you forgot, or maybe never realized you had at the time. Let me put it to you differently. What's the place of ticklers in the natural scheme of things? What's their aim in life? Their special reason? Their genius? Their final cause? What gods should ticklers worship?"

But Gusterson was already shaking his head. He said, "I don't know anything about that at all."

Fay sighed and gave simultaneously with Pooh-Bah the now-familiar triple-jointed shrug. Then the man briskened himself. "I guess that's as far as we can get right now," he said. "Keep thinking, Gussy. Try to remember something. You won't be able to leave your apartment — I'm setting guards. If you want to see me, tell them. Or just think — In due course you'll be questioned further in any case. Perhaps by special methods. Perhaps you'll be ticklerized. That's all. Come on, everybody, let's get going."

The pimply woman and her pal let go of Gusterson, Daisy's man loosed his decorous hold, Davidson and Kester sidled away with an eye behind them and the little storm troop trudged out.

Fay looked back in the doorway. "I'm sorry, Gussy," he said and for a moment his old self looked out of his eyes. "I wish I could —" A claw reached for his ear, a spasm of pain crossed his face, he stiffened and marched off. The door shut.

Gusterson took two deep breaths that were close to angry sobs. Then, still breathing stentorously, he stamped into the bedroom.

"What —?" Daisy asked, looking after him.

He came back carrying his .38 and headed for the door.

"What are you up to?" she demanded, knowing very well.

"I'm going to blast that iron monkey off Fay's back if it's the last thing I do!"

She threw her arms around him.

"Now lemme go," Gusterson growled. "I gotta be a man

one time anyway."

As they struggled for the gun, the door opened noiselessly, Davidson slipped in and deftly snatched the weapon out of their hands before they realized he was there. He said nothing, only smiled at them and shook his head in sad reproof as he went out.

Gusterson slumped. "I *knew* they were all psionic," he said softly. "I just got out of control now — that last look Fay gave us." He touched Daisy's arm. "Thanks, kid."

He walked to the glass wall and looked out desultorily. After a while he turned and said, "Maybe you better be with the kids, hey? I imagine the guards'll let you through."

Daisy shook her head. "The kids never come home until supper. For the next few hours they'll be safer without me."

Gusterson nodded vaguely, sat down on the couch and propped his chin on the base of his palm. After a while his brow smoothed and Daisy knew that the wheels had started to turn inside and the electrons to jump around — except that she reminded herself to permanently cross out those particular figures of speech from her vocabulary.

After about half an hour Gusterson said softly, "I think the ticklers are so psionic that it's as if they just had one mind. If I were with them very long I'd start to be part of that mind. Say something to one of them and you say it to all."

Fifteen minutes later: "They're not crazy, they're just newborn. The ones that were creating a cootching chaos downstairs were like babies kickin' their legs and wavin' their eyes, tryin' to see what their bodies could do. Too bad their bodies are us."

Ten minutes more: "I gotta do something about it. Fay's right. It's all my fault. He's just the apprentice; I'm the old sorcerer himself."

Five minutes more, gloomily: "Maybe it's man's destiny to build live machines and then bow out of the cosmic picture. Except the ticklers need us, dammit, just like nomads need horses."

Another five minutes: "Maybe somebody could dream up a purpose in life for ticklers. Even a religion — the First Church of Pooh-Bah Tickler. But I hate selling other people spiritual ideas and that'd still leave ticklers parasitic on humans. . . ."

As he murmured those last words Gusterson's eyes got wide as a maniac's and a big smile reached for his ears. He stood up and faced himself toward the door.

"What are you intending to do now?" Daisy asked flatly.

"I'm merely goin' out an' save the world," he told her. "I may be back for supper and I may not."

VIII

Davidson pushed out from the wall against which he'd been resting himself and his two-stone tickler and moved to block the hall. But Gusterson simply walked up to him. He shook his hand warmly and looked his tickler full in the eye and said in a ringing voice, "Ticklers should have bodies of their own!" He paused and then added casually, "Come on, let's visit your boss."

Davidson listened for instructions and then nodded. But he watched Gusterson warily as they walked down the hall.

In the elevator Gusterson repeated his message to the second guard, who turned out to be the pimply woman, now wearing shoes. This time he added, "Ticklers shouldn't be tied to the frail bodies of humans, which need a lot of thoughtful supervision and drug-injecting and can't even fly."

Crossing the park, Gusterson stopped a hump-backed soldier and informed him, "Ticklers gotta cut the apron string and snap the silver cord and go out in the universe and find their own purposes." Davidson and the pimply woman didn't interfere. They merely waited and watched and then led Gusterson on.

On the escaladder he told someone, "It's cruel to tie ticklers to slow-witted snaily humans when ticklers can think and live . . . ten thousand times as fast," he finished, plucking the figure from the murk of his unconscious.

By the time they got to the bottom, the message had become, "Ticklers should have a planet of their own!"

They never did catch up with Fay, although they spent two hours skimming around on slidewalks, under the subterranean stars, pursuing rumors of his presence. Clearly the boss tickler (which was how they thought of Pooh-bah) led an energetic life. Gusterson continued to deliver his message to all and sundry at 30-second intervals. Toward the end he found himself doing it in a dreamy and forgetful way. His mind, he decided, was becoming assimilated to the communal telepathic mind of the ticklers. It did not seem to matter at the time.

After two hours Gusterson realized that he and his guides were becoming part of a general movement of people, a flow as mindless as that of blood corpuscles through the veins, yet at the same time dimly purposeful — at least there was the feeling that it was at the behest of a mind far above.

The flow was topside. All the slidewalks seemed to lead to the concourses and the escaladders. Gusterson found himself part of a human stream moving into the tickler factory adjacent to his apartment — or another factory very much like it.

Thereafter Gusterson's awarenesses were dimmed. It was as if a bigger mind were doing the remembering for him and it were permissible and even mandatory for him to dream his way along. He knew vaguely that days were passing. He knew he had work of a sort: at one time he was bringing food to gaunt-eyed tickler-mounted humans working feverishly in a production line — human hands and tickler claws working together in a blur of rapidity on silvery mechanisms that moved along jumpily on a great belt; at another he was sweeping piles of metal scraps and garbage down a gray corridor.

Two scenes stood out a little more vividly.

A windowless wall had been knocked out for twenty feet. There was blue sky outside, its light almost hurtful, and a drop of many stories. A file of humans were being processed. When one of them got to the head of the file his (or her) tickler was ceremoniously unstrapped from his shoulder and welded onto a silvery cask with smoothly pointed ends. The result was something that looked — at least in the case of the Mark 6 ticklers — like a stubby silver submarine, child size. It would hum gently, lift off the floor and then fly slowly out through the big blue gap. Then the next tickler-ridden human would step forward for processing.

The second scene was in a park, the sky again blue, but big and high with an argosy of white clouds. Gusterson was lined up in a crowd of humans that stretched as far as he could see, row on irregular row. Martial music was playing. Overhead hovered a flock of little silver submarines, lined up rather more orderly in the air than the humans were on the ground. The music rose to a heart-quickening climax. The tickler nearest Gusterson gave (as if to say, "And now — who knows?") a triple-jointed shrug that stung his memory. Then the ticklers took off straight up on their new and shining bodies. They became a flight of silver geese . . . of silver midges . . . and the humans around Gusterson lifted a ragged cheer. . . .

That scene marked the beginning of the return of Gusterson's mind and memory. He shuffled around for a bit, spoke vaguely to three or four people he recalled from the dream days, and then headed for home and supper — three weeks late, and as disoriented and emaciated as a bear coming out of hibernation.

Six months later Fay was having dinner with Daisy and Gusterson. The cocktails had been poured and the children were playing in the next apartment. The transparent violet walls brightened, then gloomed, as the sun dipped below the horizon.

Gusterson said, "I see where a spaceship out beyond the orbit of Mars was holed by a tickler. I wonder where the little guys are headed now?"

Fay started to give a writhing left-armed shrug, but stopped himself with a grimace.

"Maybe out of the solar system altogether," suggested Daisy, who'd recently dyed her hair fire-engine red and was wearing red leotards.

"They got a weary trip ahead of them," Gusterson said, "unless they work out a hyper-Einsteinian drive on the way."

Fay grimaced again. He was still looking rather peaked. He said plaintively, "Haven't we heard enough about ticklers for a while?"

"I guess so," Gusterson agreed, "but I get to wondering about the little guys. They were so serious and intense about everything. I never did solve their problem, you know. I just shifted it onto other shoulders than ours. No joke intended," he hurried to add.

Fay forbore to comment. "By the way, Gussy," he said, "have you heard anything from the Red Cross about that world-saving medal I nominated you for? I know you think the whole concept of world-saving medals is ridiculous, especially when they started giving them to all heads of state who didn't start atomic wars while in office, but —"

"Nary a peep," Gusterson told him. "I'm not proud, Fay. I could use a few world-savin' medals. I'd start a flurry in the old-gold market. But I don't worry about those things. I don't have time to. I'm busy these days thinkin' up a bunch of new inventions."

"Gussy!" Fay said sharply, his face tightening in alarm, "Have you forgotten your promise?"

"'Course not, Fay. My new inventions aren't for Micro or any other firm. They're just a legitimate part of my literary endeavors. Happens my next insanity novel is goin' to be about a mad inventor."

BREAD OVERHEAD

As a blisteringly hot but guaranteed weather-controlled future summer day dawned on the Mississippi Valley, the walking mills of Puffy Products ("Spike to Loaf in One Operation!") began to tread delicately on their centipede legs across the wheat fields of Kansas.

The walking mills resembled fat metal serpents, rather larger than those Chinese paper dragons animated by files of men in procession. Sensory robot devices in their noses informed them that the waiting wheat had reached ripe perfection.

As they advanced, their heads swung lazily from side to side, very much like snakes, gobbling the yellow grain. In their throats, it was threshed, the chaff bundled and burped aside for pickup by the crawl trucks of a chemical corporation, the kernels quick-dried and blown along into the mighty chests of the machines. There the tireless mills ground the kernels to flour, which was instantly sifted, the bran being packaged and dropped like the chaff for pickup. A cluster of tanks which gave the metal serpents a decidedly humpbacked appearance added water, shortening, salt and other ingredients, some named and some not. The dough was at the same time infused with gas from a tank conspicuously labeled "Carbon Dioxide" ("No Yeast Creatures in Your Bread!").

Thus instantly risen, the dough was clipped into loaves and shot into radionic ovens forming the midsections of the metal serpents. There the bread was baked in a matter of seconds, a fierce heat-front browning the crusts, and the piping-hot loaves sealed in transparent plastic bearing the proud Puffyloaf emblem (two cherubs circling a floating loaf) and ejected onto the delivery platform at each serpent's rear end, where a cluster of pickup machines, like hungry piglets, snatched at the loaves with hygienic claws.

A few loaves would be hurried off for the day's consumption, the majority stored for winter in strategically located mammoth deep freezes.

But now, behold a wonder! As loaves began to appear on the delivery platform of the first walking mill to get into action, they did not linger on the conveyor belt, but rose gently into the air and slowly traveled off down-wind across the hot rippling fields.

The robot claws of the pickup machines clutched in vain, and, not noticing the difference, proceeded carefully to stack emptiness, tier by tier. One errant loaf, rising more sluggishly than its fellows, was snagged by a thrusting claw. The machine paused, clumsily wiped off the injured loaf, set it aside — where it bobbed on one corner, unable to take off again — and went back to the work of storing nothingness.

A flock of crows rose from the trees of a nearby shelterbelt as the flight of loaves approached. The crows swooped to investigate and then suddenly scattered, screeching in panic.

The helicopter of a hangoverish Sunday traveler bound for Wichita shied very similarly from the brown fliers and did not return for a second look.

A black-haired housewife spied them over her back fence, crossed herself and grabbed her walkie-talkie from the laundry basket. Seconds later, the yawning correspondent of a regional newspaper was jotting down the lead of a humorous news story which, recalling the old flying-saucer scares, stated that now apparently bread was to be included in the mad aerial tea party.

The congregation of an open-walled country church, standing up to recite the most familiar of Christian prayers, had just reached the petition for daily sustenance, when a sub-flight of the loaves, either forced down by a vagrant wind or lacking the natural buoyancy of the rest, came coasting silently as the sunbeams between the graceful pillars at the altar end of the building.

Meanwhile, the main flight, now augmented by other

bread flocks from scores and hundreds of walking mills that had started work a little later, mounted slowly and majestically into the cirrus-flecked upper air, where a steady wind was blowing strongly toward the east.

About one thousand miles farther on in that direction, where a cluster of stratosphere-tickling towers marked the location of the metropolis of NewNew York, a tender scene was being enacted in the pressurized penthouse managerial suite of Puffy Products. Megera Winterly, Secretary in Chief to the Managerial Board and referred to by her underlings as the Blonde Icicle, was dealing with the advances of Roger ("Racehorse") Snedden, Assistant Secretary to the Board and often indistinguishable from any passing office boy.

"Why don't you jump out the window, Roger, remembering to shut the airlock after you?" the Golden Glacier said in tones not unkind. "When are your high-strung, thoroughbred nerves going to accept the fact that I would never consider marriage with a business inferior? You have about as much chance as a starving Ukrainian kulak now that Moscow's clapped on the interdict."

Roger's voice was calm, although his eyes were feverishly bright, as he replied, "A lot of things are going to be different around here, Meg, as soon as the Board is forced to admit that only my quick thinking made it possible to bring the name of Puffyloaf in front of the whole world."

"Puffyloaf could do with a little of that," the business girl observed judiciously. "The way sales have been plummeting, it won't be long before the Government deeds our desks to the managers of Fairy Bread and asks us to take the Big Jump. But just where does your quick thinking come into this, Mr. Snedden? You can't be referring to the helium — that was Rose Thinker's brainwave."

She studied him suspiciously. "You've birthed another promotional bumble, Roger. I can see it in your eyes. I only hope it's not as big a one as when you put the Martian ambassador on 3D and he thanked you profusely for the gross of

Puffyloaves, assuring you that he'd never slept on a softer mattress in all his life on two planets."

"Listen to me, Meg. Today — yes, today! — you're going to see the Board eating out of my hand."

"Hah! I guarantee you won't have any fingers left. You're bold enough now, but when Mr. Gryce and those two big machines come through that door —"

"Now wait a minute, Meg —"

"Hush! They're coming now!"

Roger leaped three feet in the air, but managed to land without a sound and edged toward his stool. Through the dilating iris of the door strode Phineas T. Gryce, flanked by Rose Thinker and Tin Philosopher.

The man approached the conference table in the center of the room with measured pace and gravely expressionless face. The rose-tinted machine on his left did a couple of impulsive pirouettes on the way and twittered a greeting to Meg and Roger. The other machine quietly took the third of the high seats and lifted a claw at Meg, who now occupied a stool twice the height of Roger's.

"Miss Winterly, please — our theme."

The Blonde Icicle's face thawed into a little-girl smile as she chanted bubblingly:

> *"Made up of tiny wheaten motes*
> *And reinforced with sturdy oats,*
> *It rises through the air and floats —*
> *The bread on which all Terra dotes!"*

"Thank you, Miss Winterly," said Tin Philosopher. "Though a purely figurative statement, that bit about rising through the air always gets me — here." He rapped his mid-section, which gave off a high musical *clang*.

"Ladies —" he inclined his photocells toward Rose Thinker and Meg — "and gentlemen. This is a historic occasion in Old Puffy's long history, the inauguration of the helium-filled loaf ('So Light It Almost Floats Away!') in which that inert and heaven-aspiring gas replaces old-fashioned carbon dioxide. Later, there will be kudos for Rose Thinker, whose bright relays genius-sparked the idea, and also for Roger Snedden, who took care of the details.

"By the by, Racehorse, that was a brilliant piece of work getting the helium out of the government — they've been pretty stuffy lately about their monopoly. But first I want to throw wide the casement in your minds that opens on the Long View of Things."

Rose Thinker spun twice on her chair and opened her photocells wide. Tin Philosopher coughed to limber up the diaphragm of his speaker and continued:

"Ever since the first cave wife boasted to her next-den neighbor about the superior paleness and fluffiness of her tortillas, mankind has sought lighter, whiter bread. Indeed, thinkers wiser than myself have equated the whole upward course of culture with this poignant quest. Yeast was a wonderful discovery — for its primitive day. Sifting the bran and wheat germ from the flour was an even more important advance. Early bleaching and preserving chemicals played their humble parts.

"For a while, barbarous faddists — blind to the deeply spiritual nature of bread, which is recognized by all great religions — held back our march toward perfection with their hair-splitting insistence on the vitamin content of the wheat germ, but their case collapsed when tasteless colorless substitutes were triumphantly synthesized and introduced into the loaf, which for flawless purity, unequaled airiness and sheer intangible goodness was rapidly becoming mankind's supreme gustatory experience."

"I wonder what the stuff tastes like," Rose Thinker said out of a clear sky.

"I wonder what taste tastes like," Tin Philosopher echoed dreamily. Recovering himself, he continued:

"Then, early in the twenty-first century, came the epochal researches of Everett Whitehead, Puffyloaf chemist, culminating in his paper 'The Structural Bubble in Cereal Masses' and making possible the baking of airtight bread twenty times stronger (for its weight) than steel and of a lightness that would have been incredible even to the advanced chemist-bakers of the twentieth century — a lightness so great that, besides forming the backbone of our own promotion, it has forever since been capitalized on by our conscienceless competitors of Fairy Bread with their enduring slogan: 'It Makes Ghost Toast'."

"That's a beaut, all right, that ecto-dough blurb," Rose Thinker admitted, bugging her photocells sadly. "Wait a sec. How about? —

> *"There'll be bread*
> *Overhead*
> *When you're dead —*
> *It is said."*

Phineas T. Gryce wrinkled his nostrils at the pink machine as if he smelled her insulation smoldering. He said mildly, "A somewhat unhappy jingle, Rose, referring as it does to the end of the customer as consumer. Moreover, we shouldn't overplay the figurative 'rises through the air' angle. What inspired you?"

She shrugged. "I don't know — oh, yes, I do. I was remembering one of the workers' songs we machines used to chant during the Big Strike —

> *"Work and pray,*
> *Live on hay.*
> *You'll get pie*
> *In the sky*
> *When you die —*
> *It's a lie!*

"I don't know why we chanted it," she added. "We didn't want pie — or hay, for that matter. And machines don't pray, except Tibetan prayer wheels."

Phineas T. Gryce shook his head. "Labor relations are another topic we should stay far away from. However, dear Rose, I'm glad you keep trying to outjingle those dirty crooks at Fairy Bread." He scowled, turning back his attention to Tin Philosopher. "I get whopping mad, Old Machine, whenever I hear that other slogan of theirs, the discriminatory one — 'Untouched by Robot Claws.' Just because they employ a few filthy androids in their factories!"

Tin Philosopher lifted one of his own sets of bright talons. "Thanks, P.T. But to continue my historical resume, the next great advance in the baking art was the substitution of purified carbon dioxide, recovered from coal smoke, for the gas generated by yeast organisms indwelling in the dough and later killed by the heat of baking, their corpses remaining *in situ*. But even purified carbon dioxide is itself a rather repugnant gas, a product of metabolism whether fast or slow, and forever associated with those life processes which are obnoxious to the fastidious."

Here the machine shuddered with delicate clinkings. "Therefore, we of Puffyloaf are taking today what may be the ultimate step toward purity: we are aerating our loaves with the noble gas helium, an element which remains virginal in the face of all chemical temptations and whose slim molecules are eleven times lighter than obese carbon dioxide — yes, noble uncontaminable helium, which, if it be a kind of ash, is yet the ash only of radioactive burning, accomplished or initiated entirely on the Sun, a safe 93 million miles from this planet. Let's have a cheer for the helium loaf!"

Without changing expression, Phineas T. Gryce rapped the table thrice in solemn applause, while the others bowed their heads.

"Thanks, T.P.," P.T. then said. "And now for the Moment of Truth. Miss Winterly, how is the helium loaf selling?"

The business girl clapped on a pair of earphones and whispered into a lapel mike. Her gaze grew abstracted as she mentally translated flurries of brief squawks into coherent messages. Suddenly a single vertical furrow creased her matchlessly smooth brow.

"It isn't, Mr. Gryce!" she gasped in horror. "Fairy Bread is outselling Puffyloaves by an infinity factor. So far this morning, *there has not been one single delivery of Puffyloaves to any sales spot*! Complaints about non-delivery are pouring in from both walking stores and sessile shops."

"Mr. Snedden!" Gryce barked. "What bug in the new helium process might account for this delay?"

Roger was on his feet, looking bewildered. "I can't imagine, sir, unless — just possibly — there's been some unforeseeable difficulty involving the new metal-foil wrappers."

"Metal-foil wrappers? Were *you* responsible for those?"

"Yes, sir. Last-minute recalculations showed that the extra lightness of the new loaf might be great enough to cause drift during stackage. Drafts in stores might topple sales pyramids. Metal-foil wrappers, by their added weight, took care of the difficulty."

"And you ordered them without consulting the Board?"

"Yes, sir. There was hardly time and —"

"Why, you fool! I noticed that order for metal-foil wrappers, assumed it was some sub-secretary's mistake, and canceled it last night!"

Roger Snedden turned pale. "You canceled it?" he quavered. "And told them to go back to the lighter plastic wrappers?"

"Of course! Just what is behind all this, Mr. Snedden? *What* recalculations were you trusting, when our physicists had demonstrated months ago that the helium loaf was safely stackable in light airs and gentle breezes — winds up to Beaufort's scale 3. *Why* should a change from heavier to lighter wrappers result in complete non-delivery?"

Roger Snedden's paleness became tinged with an interesting green. He cleared his throat and made strange gulping noises. Tin Philosopher's photocells focused on him calmly, Rose Thinker's with unfeigned excitement. P.T. Gryce's frown grew blacker by the moment, while Megera Winterly's Venus-mask showed an odd dawning of dismay and awe. She was getting new squawks in her earphones.

"Er . . . ah . . . er. . . ." Roger said in winning tones. "Well, you see, the fact is that I. . . ."

"Hold it," Meg interrupted crisply. "Triple-urgent from Public Relations, Safety Division. Tulsa-Topeka aero-express makes emergency landing after being buffeted in encounter with vast flight of objects first described as brown birds, although no failures reported in airway's electronic anti-bird fences. After grounding safely near Emporia — no fatalities — pilot's windshield found thinly plastered with soft white-and-brown material. Emblems on plastic wrappers embedded in material identify it incontrovertibly as an undetermined number of Puffyloaves cruising at three thousand feet!"

Eyes and photocells turned inquisitorially upon Roger Snedden. He went from green to Puffyloaf white and blurted: "All right, I did it, but it was the only way out! Yesterday morning, due to the Ukrainian crisis, the government stopped sales and deliveries of all strategic stockpiled materials, including helium gas. Puffy's new program of advertising and promotion, based on the lighter loaf, was already rolling. There was only one thing to do, there being only one other gas comparable in lightness to helium. I diverted the necessary quantity of hydrogen gas from the Hydrogenated Oils Section of our Magna-Margarine Division and substituted it for the helium."

"You substituted . . . hydrogen . . . for the . . . helium?" Phineas T. Gryce faltered in low mechanical tones, taking four steps backward.

"Hydrogen is twice as light as helium," Tin Philosopher remarked judiciously.

"And many times cheaper — did you know that?" Roger countered feebly. "Yes, I substituted hydrogen. The metal-foil wrapping would have added just enough weight to counteract the greater buoyancy of the hydrogen loaf. But —"

"So, when this morning's loaves began to arrive on the delivery platforms of the walking mills. . . ." Tin Philosopher left the remark unfinished.

"Exactly," Roger agreed dismally.

"Let me ask you, Mr. Snedden," Gryce interjected, still in low tones, "if you expected people to jump to the kitchen ceiling for their Puffybread after taking off the metal wrapper, or reach for the sky if they happened to unwrap the stuff outdoors?"

"Mr. Gryce," Roger said reproachfully, "you have often assured me that what people do with Puffybread after they buy it is no concern of ours."

"I seem to recall," Rose Thinker chirped somewhat unkindly, "that dictum was created to answer inquiries after Roger put the famous sculptures-in-miniature artist on 3D and he testified that he always molded his first attempts from Puffybread, one jumbo loaf squeezing down to approximately the size of a peanut."

Her photocells dimmed and brightened. "Oh, boy — hydrogen! The loaf's unwrapped. After a while, in spite of the crust-seal, a little oxygen diffuses in. An explosive mixture. Housewife in curlers and kimono pops a couple slices in the toaster. Boom!"

The three human beings in the room winced.

Tin Philosopher kicked her under the table, while observing, "So you see, Roger, that the non-delivery of the hydrogen loaf carries some consolations. And I must confess that one aspect of the affair gives me great satisfaction, not as a Board Member but as a private machine. You have at last made a reality of the 'rises through the air' part of Puffybread's theme. They can't ever take that away from you. By now, half the inhabitants of the Great Plains must have observed our flying loaves rising high."

Phineas T. Gryce shot a frightened look at the west windows and found his full voice.

"Stop the mills!" he roared at Meg Winterly, who nodded and whispered urgently into her mike.

"A sensible suggestion," Tin Philosopher said. "But it comes a trifle late in the day. If the mills are still walking and grinding, approximately seven billion Puffyloaves are at this moment cruising eastward over Middle America. Remember that a six-month supply for deep-freeze is involved and that the current consumption of bread, due to its matchless airiness, is eight and one-half loaves per person per day."

Phineas T. Gryce carefully inserted both hands into his scanty hair, feeling for a good grip. He leaned menacingly toward Roger who, chin resting on the table, regarded him apathetically.

"Hold it!" Meg called sharply. "Flock of multiple-urgents coming in. News Liaison: information bureaus swamped with flying-bread inquiries. Aero-expresslines: Clear our airways or face law suit. U. S. Army: Why do loaves flame when hit by incendiary bullets? U. S. Customs: If bread intended for export, get export license or face prosecution. Russian Consulate in Chicago: Advise on destination of bread-lift. And some Kansas church is accusing us of a hoax inciting to blasphemy, of faking miracles — I don't know *why.*"

The business girl tore off her headphones. "Roger Snedden," she cried with a hysteria that would have dumfounded her underlings, "you've brought the name of Puffyloaf in front of the whole world, all right! Now do something about the situation!"

Roger nodded obediently. But his pallor increased a shade, the pupils of his eyes disappeared under the upper lids, and his head burrowed beneath his forearms.

"Oh, boy," Rose Thinker called gayly to Tin Philosopher, "this looks like the start of a real crisis session! Did you remember to bring spare batteries?"

Meanwhile, the monstrous flight of Puffyloaves, filling midwestern skies as no small fliers had since the days of the passenger pigeon, soared steadily onward.

Private fliers approached the brown and glistening bread-front in curiosity and dipped back in awe. Aero-expresslines organized sightseeing flights along the flanks. Planes of the government forestry and agricultural services and 'copters bearing the Puffyloaf emblem hovered on the fringes, watching developments and waiting for orders. A squadron of supersonic fighters hung menacingly above.

The behavior of birds varied considerably. Most fled or gave the loaves a wide berth, but some bolder species, discovering the minimal nutritive nature of the translucent brown objects, attacked them furiously with beaks and claws. Hydrogen diffusing slowly through the crusts had now distended most of the sealed plastic wrappers into little balloons, which ruptured, when pierced, with disconcerting *pops*.

Below, neck-craning citizens crowded streets and back yards, cranks and cultists had a field day, while local and national governments raged indiscriminately at Puffyloaf and at each other.

Rumors that a fusion weapon would be exploded in the midst of the flying bread drew angry protests from conservationists and a flood of telefax pamphlets titled "H-Loaf or H-bomb?"

Stockholm sent a mystifying note of praise to the United Nations Food Organization.

Delhi issued nervous denials of a millet blight that no one had heard of until that moment and reaffirmed India's ability to feed her population with no outside help except the usual.

Radio Moscow asserted that the Kremlin would brook no interference in its treatment of the Ukrainians, jokingly referred to the flying bread as a farce perpetrated by mad internationalists inhabiting Cloud Cuckoo Land, added contradictory references to airborne bread booby-trapped by Capitalist gangsters, and then fell moodily silent on the whole topic.

Radio Venus reported to its winged audience that Earth's

inhabitants were establishing food depots in the upper air, preparatory to taking up permanent aerial residence "such as we have always enjoyed on Venus."

NewNew York made feverish preparations for the passage of the flying bread. Tickets for sightseeing space in skyscrapers were sold at high prices; cold meats and potted spreads were hawked to viewers with the assurance that they would be able to snag the bread out of the air and enjoy a historic sandwich.

Phineas T. Gryce, escaping from his own managerial suite, raged about the city, demanding general cooperation in the stretching of great nets between the skyscrapers to trap the errant loaves. He was captured by Tin Philosopher, escaped again, and was found posted with oxygen mask and submachine gun on the topmost spire of Puffyloaf Tower, apparently determined to shoot down the loaves as they appeared and before they involved his company in more trouble with Customs and the State Department.

Recaptured by Tin Philosopher, who suffered only minor bullet holes, he was given a series of mild electroshocks and returned to the conference table, calm and clear-headed as ever.

But the bread flight, swinging away from a hurricane moving up the Atlantic coast, crossed a clouded-in Boston by night and disappeared into a high Atlantic overcast, also thereby evading a local storm generated by the Weather Department in a last-minute effort to bring down or at least disperse the H-loaves.

Warnings and counterwarnings by Communist and Capitalist governments seriously interfered with military trailing of the flight during this period and it was actually lost in touch with for several days.

At scattered points, seagulls were observed fighting over individual loaves floating down from the gray roof — that was all.

A mood of spirituality strongly tinged with humor seized

the people of the world. Ministers sermonized about the bread, variously interpreting it as a call to charity, a warning against gluttony, a parable of the evanescence of all earthly things, and a divine joke. Husbands and wives, facing each other across their walls of breakfast toast, burst into laughter. The mere sight of a loaf of bread anywhere was enough to evoke guffaws. An obscure sect, having as part of its creed the injunction "Don't take yourself so damn seriously," won new adherents.

The bread flight, rising above an Atlantic storm widely reported to have destroyed it, passed unobserved across a foggy England and rose out of the overcast only over Mittel-europa. The loaves had at last reached their maximum altitude.

The Sun's rays beat through the rarified air on the distended plastic wrappers, increasing still further the pressure of the confined hydrogen. They burst by the millions and tens of millions. A high-flying Bulgarian evangelist, who had happened to mistake the up-lever for the east-lever in the cockpit of his flier and who was the sole witness of the event, afterward described it as "the foaming of a sea of diamonds, the crackle of God's knuckles."

By the millions and tens of millions, the loaves coasted down into the starving Ukraine. Shaken by a week of humor that threatened to invade even its own grim precincts, the Kremlin made a sudden about-face. A new policy was instituted of communal ownership of the produce of communal farms, and teams of hunger-fighters and caravans of trucks loaded with pumpernickel were dispatched into the Ukraine.

World distribution was given to a series of photographs showing peasants queueing up to trade scavenged Puffy-loaves for traditional black bread, recently aerated itself but still extra solid by comparison, the rate of exchange demanded by the Moscow teams being twenty Puffyloaves to one of pumpernickel.

Another series of photographs, picturing chubby workers' children being blown to bits by booby-trapped bread, was quietly destroyed.

Congratulatory notes were exchanged by various national governments and world organizations, including the Brotherhood of Free Business Machines. The great bread flight was over, though for several weeks afterward scattered falls of loaves occurred, giving rise to a new folklore of manna among lonely Arabian tribesmen, and in one well-authenticated instance in Tibet, sustaining life in a party of mountaineers cut off by a snow slide.

Back in NewNew York, the managerial board of Puffy Products slumped in utter collapse around the conference table, the long crisis session at last ended. Empty coffee cartons were scattered around the chairs of the three humans, dead batteries around those of the two machines. For a while, there was no movement whatsoever. Then Roger Snedden reached out wearily for the earphones where Megera Winterly had hurled them down, adjusted them to his head, pushed a button and listened apathetically.

After a bit, his gaze brightened. He pushed more buttons and listened more eagerly. Soon he was sitting tensely upright on his stool, eyes bright and lower face all a-smile, muttering terse comments and questions into the lapel mike torn from Meg's fair neck.

The others, reviving, watched him, at first dully, then with quickening interest, especially when he jerked off the earphones with a happy shout and sprang to his feet.

"Listen to this!" he cried in a ringing voice. "As a result of the worldwide publicity, Puffyloaves are outselling Fairy Bread three to one — and that's just the old carbon-dioxide stock from our freezers! It's almost exhausted, but the government, now that the Ukrainian crisis is over, has taken the ban off helium and will also sell us stockpiled wheat if we need it. We can have our walking mills burrowing into the wheat caves in a matter of hours!

"But that isn't all! The far greater demand everywhere is for Puffyloaves that will actually float. Public Relations, Child Liaison Division, reports that the kiddies are making their mothers' lives miserable about it. If only we can figure out some way to make hydrogen non-explosive or the helium loaf float just a little —"

"I'm sure we can take care of that quite handily," Tin Philosopher interrupted briskly. "Puffyloaf has kept it a corporation secret — even you've never been told about it — but just before he went crazy, Everett Whitehead discovered a way to make bread using only half as much flour as we do in the present loaf. Using this secret technique, which we've been saving for just such an emergency, it will be possible to bake a helium loaf as buoyant in every respect as the hydrogen loaf."

"Good!" Roger cried. "We'll tether 'em on strings and sell 'em like balloons. No mother-child shopping team will leave the store without a cluster. Buying bread balloons will be the big event of the day for kiddies. It'll make the carry-home shopping load lighter too! I'll issue orders at once —"

He broke off, looking at Phineas T. Gryce, said with quiet assurance, "Excuse me, sir, if I seem to be taking too much upon myself."

"Not at all, son; go straight ahead," the great manager said approvingly. "You're" — he laughed in anticipation of getting off a memorable remark — "rising to the challenging situation like a genuine Puffyloaf."

Megera Winterly looked from the older man to the younger. Then in a single leap she was upon Roger, her arms wrapped tightly around him.

"My sweet little ever-victorious, self-propelled monkey wrench!" she crooned in his ear. Roger looked fatuously over her soft shoulder at Tin Philosopher who, as if moved by some similar feeling, reached over and touched claws with Rose Thinker.

This, however, was what he telegraphed silently to his fellow machine across the circuit so completed:

"Good-o, Rosie! That makes another victory for robot-engineered world unity, though you almost gave us away at the start with that 'bread overhead' jingle. We've struck another blow against the next world war, in which — as we know only too well! — we machines would suffer the most. Now if we can only arrange, say, a fur-famine in Alaska and a migration of long-haired Siberian lemmings across Behring Straits . . . we'd have to swing the Japanese Current up there so it'd be warm enough for the little fellows. . . . Anyhow, Rosie, with a spot of help from the Brotherhood, those humans will paint themselves into the peace corner yet."

Meanwhile, he and Rose Thinker quietly watched the Blonde Icicle melt.

NO GREAT MAGIC

I

To bring the dead to life
Is no great magic.
Few are wholly dead:
Blow on a dead man's embers
And a live flame will start.
— Graves

I dipped through the filmy curtain into the boys' half of the dressing room and there was Sid sitting at the star's dressing table in his threadbare yellowed undershirt, the lucky one, not making up yet but staring sternly at himself in the bulb-framed mirror and experimentally working his features a little, as actors will, and kneading the stubble on his fat chin.

I said to him quietly, "Siddy, what are we putting on tonight? Maxwell Anderson's *Elizabeth the Queen* or Shakespeare's *Macbeth*? It says *Macbeth* on the callboard, but Miss Nefer's getting ready for Elizabeth. She just had me go and fetch the red wig."

He tried out a few eyebrow rears — right, left, both together — then turned to me, sucking in his big gut a little, as he always does when a gal heaves into hailing distance, and said, "Your pardon, sweetling, what sayest thou?"

Sid always uses that kook antique patter backstage, until I sometimes wonder whether I'm in Central Park, New York City, nineteen hundred and three quarters, or somewhere in Southwark, Merry England, fifteen hundred and same. The truth is that although he loves every last fat part in Shakespeare and will play the skinniest one with loyal and inspired affection, he thinks Willy S. penned Falstaff with nobody else in mind but Sidney J. Lessingham. (And no accent on the ham, please.)

I closed my eyes and counted to eight, then repeated my

question.

He replied, "Why, the Bard's tragical history of the bloody Scot, certes." He waved his hand toward the portrait of Shakespeare that always sits beside his mirror on top of his reserve makeup box. At first that particular picture of the Bard looked too nancy to me — a sort of peeping-tom school-teacher — but I've grown used to it over the months and even palsy-feeling.

He didn't ask me why I hadn't asked Miss Nefer my question. Everybody in the company knows she spends the hour before curtain-time getting into character, never parting her lips except for that purpose — or to bite your head off if you try to make the most necessary conversation.

"Aye, 'tiz *Macbeth* tonight," Sid confirmed, returning to his frowning-practice: left eyebrow up, right down, reverse, repeat, rest. "And I must play the ill-starred Thane of Glamis."

I said, "That's fine, Siddy, but where does it leave us with Miss Nefer? She's already thinned her eyebrows and beaked out the top of her nose for Queen Liz, though that's as far as she's got. A beautiful job, the nose. Anybody else would think it was plastic surgery instead of putty. But it's going to look kind of funny on the Thaness of Glamis."

Sid hesitated a half second longer than he usually would — I thought, *his timing's off tonight* — and then he harrumphed and said, "Why, Iris Nefer, decked out as Good Queen Bess, will speak a prologue to the play — a prologue which I have myself but last week writ." He owled his eyes. "'Tis an experiment in the new theater."

I said, "Siddy, prologues were nothing new to Shakespeare. He had them on half his other plays. Besides, it doesn't make sense to use Queen Elizabeth. She was dead by the time he whipped up *Macbeth*, which is all about witch-craft and directed at King James."

He growled a little at me and demanded, "Prithee, how comes it your peewit-brain bears such a ballast of fusty book-knowledge, chit?"

I said softly, "Siddy, you don't camp in a Shakespearean dressing room for a year, tete-a-teting with some of the wisest actors ever, without learning a little. Sure I'm a mental case, a poor little A & A existing on your sweet charity, and don't think I don't appreciate it, but —"

"A-*and*-A, thou sayest?" he frowned. "Methinks the gladsome new forswearers of sack and ale call themselves AA."

"Agoraphobe and Amnesiac," I told him. "But look, Siddy, I was going to sayest that I do know the plays. Having Queen Elizabeth speak a prologue to *Macbeth* is as much an anachronism as if you put her on the gantry of the British moonship, busting a bottle of champagne over its schnozzle."

"Ha!" he cried as if he'd caught me out. "And saying there's a new Elizabeth, wouldn't that be the bravest advertisement ever for the Empire? — perchance rechristening the pilot, copilot and astrogator Drake, Hawkins and Raleigh? And the ship *The Golden Hind*? Tilly fally, lady!"

He went on, "My prologue an anachronism, quotha! The groundlings will never mark it. Think'st thou wisdom came to mankind with the stenchful rocket and the sundered atomy? More, the Bard himself was topfull of anachronism. He put spectacles on King Lear, had clocks tolling the hour in Caesar's Rome, buried that Roman 'stead o' burning him and gave Czechoslovakia a seacoast. Go to, doll."

"Czechoslovakia, Siddy?"

"Bohemia, then, what skills it? Leave me now, sweet poppet. Go thy ways. I have matters of import to ponder. There's more to running a repertory company than reading the footnotes to Furness."

Martin had just slouched by calling the Half Hour and looking in his solemnity, sneakers, levis and dirty T-shirt more like an underage refugee from Skid Row than Sid's newest recruit, assistant stage manager and hardest-worked juvenile — though for once he'd remembered to shave. I was about to ask Sid who was going to play Lady Mack if Miss

Nefer wasn't, or, if she were going to double the roles, shouldn't I help her with the change? She's a slow dresser and the Elizabeth costumes are pretty realistically stayed. And she would have trouble getting off that nose, I was sure. But then I saw that Siddy was already slapping on the alboline to keep the grease paint from getting into his pores.

Greta, you ask too many questions, I told myself. You get everybody riled up and you rack your own poor ricketty little mind; and I hied myself off to the costumery to settle my nerves.

The costumery, which occupies the back end of the dressing room, is exactly the right place to settle the nerves and warm the fancies of any child, including an unraveled adult who's saving what's left of her sanity by pretending to be one. To begin with there are the regular costumes for Shakespeare's plays, all jeweled and spangled and brocaded, stage armor, great Roman togas with weights in the borders to make them drape right, velvets of every color to rest your cheek against and dream, and the fantastic costumes for the other plays we favor; Ibsen's *Peer Gynt*, Shaw's *Back to Methuselah* and Hilliard's adaptation of Heinlein's *Children of Methuselah*, the Capek brothers' *Insect People*, O'Neill's *The Fountain*, Flecker's *Hassan*, *Camino Real*, *Children of the Moon*, *The Beggar's Opera*, *Mary of Scotland*, *Berkeley Square*, *The Road to Rome*.

There are also the costumes for all the special and variety performances we give of the plays: *Hamlet* in modern dress, *Julius Caesar* set in a dictatorship of the 1920's, *The Taming of the Shrew* in caveman furs and leopard skins, where Petruchio comes in riding a dinosaur, *The Tempest* set on another planet with a spaceship wreck to start it off *Karrumph!* — which means a half dozen spacesuits, featherweight but looking ever so practical, and the weirdest sort of extraterrestrial-beast outfits for Ariel and Caliban and the other monsters.

Oh, I tell you the stuff in the costumery ranges over such a sweep of space and time that you sometimes get frightened you'll be whirled up and spun off just anywhere, so that you have to clutch at something very real to you to keep it from happening and to remind you where you *really* are — as I did now at the subway token on the thin gold chain around my neck (Siddy's first gift to me that I can remember) and chanted very softly to myself, like a charm or a prayer, closing my eyes and squeezing the holes in the token: "Columbus Circle, Times Square, Penn Station, Christopher Street. . . ."

But you don't ever get *really* frightened in the costumery. Not exactly, though your goosehairs get wonderfully realistically tingled and your tummy chilled from time to time — because you know it's all make-believe, a lifesize doll world, a children's dress-up world. It gets you thinking of far-off times and scenes as *pleasant* places and not as black hungry mouths that might gobble you up and keep you forever. It's always safe, always *just in the theatre, just on the stage*, no matter how far it seems to plunge and roam . . . and the best sort of therapy for a pot-holed mind like mine, with as many gray ruts and curves and gaps as its cerebrum, that can't remember one single thing before this last year in the dressing room and that can't ever push its shaking body out of that same motherly fatherly room, except to stand in the wings for a scene or two and watch the play until the fear gets too great and the urge to take just one peek at *the audience* gets too strong . . . and I remember what happened the two times I *did* peek, and I have to come scuttling back.

The costumery's good occupational therapy for me, too, as my pricked and calloused fingertips testify. I think I must have stitched up or darned half the costumes in it this last twelvemonth, though there are so many of them that I swear the drawers have accordion pleats and the racks extend into the fourth dimension — not to mention the boxes of props and the shelves of scripts and prompt-copies and other books, including a couple of encyclopedias and the many thick volumes of Furness's *Variorum Shakespeare*, which as Sid had guessed I'd been boning up on. Oh, and I've sponged and pressed enough costumes, too, and even refitted them to newcomers like Martin, ripping up and resewing seams, which can be a punishing job with heavy materials.

In a less sloppily organized company I'd be called wardrobe mistress, I guess. Except that to anyone in show business that suggests a crotchety old dame with lots of authority and scissors hanging around her neck on a string. Although I got my crochets, all right, I'm not that old. Kind of childish, in fact. As for authority, everybody outranks me, even Martin.

Of course to somebody *outside* show business, wardrobe mistress might suggest a yummy gal who spends her time dressing up as Nell Gwyn or Anitra or Mrs. Pinchwife or Cleopatra or even Eve (we got a legal costume for it) and inspiring the boys. I've tried that once or twice. But Siddy frowns on it, and if Miss Nefer ever caught me at it I think she'd whang me.

And in a normaller company it would be the wardrobe room, too, but costumery is my infantile name for it and the actors go along with my little whims.

I don't mean to suggest our company is completely crackers. To get as close to Broadway even as Central Park you got to have something. But in spite of Sid's whip-cracking there is a comforting looseness about its efficiency — people trade around the parts they play without fuss, the bill may be changed a half hour before curtain without anybody getting hysterics, nobody gets fired for eating garlic and breathing it in the leading lady's face. In short, we're a team. Which is funny when you come to think of it, as Sid and Miss Nefer and Bruce and Maudie are British (Miss Nefer with a touch of Eurasian blood, I romance); Martin and Beau and me are American (at least I *think* I am) while the rest come from just everywhere.

Besides my costumery work, I fetch things and run inside errands and help the actresses dress and the actors too. The dressing room's very coeducational in a halfway respectable way. And every once in a while Martin and I police up the whole place, me skittering about with dustcloth and waste-basket, he wielding the scrub-brush and mop with such silent grim efficiency that it always makes me nervous to get through and duck back into the costumery to collect myself.

Yes, the costumery's a great place to quiet your nerves or improve your mind or even dream your life away. But this time I couldn't have been there eight minutes when Miss Nefer's Elizabeth-angry voice came skirling, "Girl! Girl! Greta, where is my ruff with silver trim?" I laid my hands on it in a flash and loped it to her, because Old Queen Liz was known to slap even her Maids of Honor around a bit now and then and Miss Nefer is a bear on getting into character — a real Paul Muni.

She was all made up now, I was happy to note, at least as far as her face went — I hate to see that spooky eight-spoked faint tattoo on her forehead (I've sometimes wondered if she got it acting in India or Egypt maybe).

Yes, she was already all made up. This time she'd been going extra heavy on the burrowing-into-character bit, I could tell right away, even if it was only for a hacked-out anachronistic prologue. She signed to me to help her dress without even looking at me, but as I got busy I looked at *her* eyes. They were so cold and sad and lonely (maybe because they were so far away from her eyebrows and temples and small tight mouth, and so shut away from each other by that ridge of nose) that I got the creeps. Then she began to mur-mur and sigh, very softly at first, then loudly enough so I got the sense of it.

"Cold, so cold," she said, still seeing things far away though her hands were working smoothly with mine. "Even a gallop hardly fires my blood. Never was such a Januarius, though there's no snow. Snow will not come, or tears. Yet my brain burns with the thought of Mary's death-warrant un-signed. There's my particular hell! — to doom, perchance, all future queens, or leave a hole for the Spaniard and the Pope to creep like old worms back into the sweet apple of England.

Philip's tall black crooked ships massing like sea-going fortresses south-away — cragged castles set to march into the waves. Parma in the Lowlands! And all the while my bright young idiot gentlemen spurting out my treasure as if it were so much water, as if gold pieces were a glut of summer posies. Oh, alackanight!"

And I thought, Cry Iced! — that's sure going to be one tyrannosaur of a prologue. And how you'll ever shift back to being Lady Mack beats me. Greta, if this is what it takes to do just a bit part, you'd better give up your secret ambition of playing walk-ons some day when your nerves heal.

She was really getting to me, you see, with that characterization. It was as if I'd managed to go out and take a walk and sat down in the park outside and heard the President talking to himself about the chances of war with Russia and realized he'd sat down on a bench with its back to mine and only a bush between. You see, here we were, two females undignifiedly twisted together, at the moment getting her into that crazy crouch-deep bodice that's like a big icecream cone, and yet here at the same time was Queen Elizabeth the First of England, three hundred and umpty-ump years dead, coming back to life in a Central Park dressing room. It shook me.

She looked so much the part, you see — even without the red wig yet, just powdered pale makeup going back to a quarter of an inch from her own short dark bang combed and netted back tight. The age too. Miss Nefer can't be a day over forty — well, forty-two at most — but now she looked and talked and felt to my hands dressing her, well, at least a dozen years older. I guess when Miss Nefer gets into character she does it with each molecule.

That age point fascinated me so much that I risked asking her a question. Probably I was figuring that she couldn't do me much damage because of the positions we happened to be in at the moment. You see, I'd started to lace her up and to do it right I had my knee against the tail of her spine.

"How old, I mean how young might your majesty be?" I

asked her, innocently wonderingly like some dumb serving wench.

For a wonder she didn't somehow swing around and clout me, but only settled into character a little more deeply.

"Fifty-four winters," she replied dismally. "'Tiz Januarius of Our Lord's year One Thousand and Five Hundred and Eighty and Seven. I sit cold in Greenwich, staring at the table where Mary's death warrant waits only my sign manual. If I send her to the block, I open the doors to future, less official regicides. But if I doom her not, Philip's armada will come inching up the Channel in a season, puffing smoke and shot, and my English Catholics, thinking only of Mary Regina, will rise and i' the end the Spaniard will have all. All history would alter. That must not be, even if I'm damned for it! And yet ... and yet. . . ."

A bright blue fly came buzzing along (the dressing room has *some* insect life) and slowly circled her head rather close, but she didn't even flicker her eyelids.

"I sit cold in Greenwich, going mad. Each afternoon I ride, praying for some mischance, some prodigy, to wash from my mind away the bloody question for some little space. It skills not what: a fire, a tree a-failing, Davison or e'en Eyes Leicester tumbled with his horse, an assassin's ball clipping the cold twigs by my ear, a maid crying rape, a wild boar charging with dipping tusks, news of the Spaniard at Thames' mouth or, more happily, a band of strolling actors setting forth some new comedy to charm the fancy or some great unheard-of tragedy to tear the heart — though that were somewhat much to hope for at this season and place, even if Southwark be close by."

The lacing was done. I stood back from her, and really she looked so much like Elizabeth painted by Gheeraerts or on the Great Seal of Ireland or something — though the ash-colored plush dress trimmed in silver and the little silver-edge ruff and the black-silver tinsel-cloth cloak lined with white plush hanging behind her looked most like a winter riding costume — and her face was such a pale frozen mask of Eliza-beth's inward tortures, that I told myself, *Oh, I got to talk to Siddy again, he's made some big mistake, the lardy old lackwit. Miss Nefer just can't be figuring on playing in Macbeth tonight.*

As a matter of fact I was nerving myself to ask *her* all about it direct, though it was going to take some real nerve and maybe be risking broken bones or at least a flayed cheek to break the ice of that characterization, when who should come by calling the Fifteen Minutes but Martin. He looked so downright goofy that it took my mind off Nefer-in-character for all of eight seconds.

His levied bottom half still looked like *The Lower Depths.* Martin is Village Stanislavsky rather than Ye Olde English Stage Traditions. But above that . . . well, all it really amounted to was that he was stripped to the waist and had shaved off the small high tuft of chest hair and was wearing a black wig that hung down in front of his shoulders in two big braids heavy with silver hoops and pins. But just the same those simple things, along with his tarpaper-solarium tan and habitual poker expression, made him look so like an American Indian that I thought, *Hey Zeus! — he's all set to play Hiawatha, or if he'd just cover up that straight-line chest, a frowny Pocahontas.* And I quick ran through what plays with Indian parts we do and could only come up with *The Fountain.*

I mutely goggled my question at him, wiggling my hands like guppy fins, but he brushed me off with a solemn myste-rious smile and backed through the curtain. I thought, *nobody can explain this but Siddy*, and I followed Martin.

II

History does not move in one current,
like the wind across bare seas,
but in a thousand streams and eddies,
like the wind over a broken landscape.
— Cary

The boys' half of the dressing room (two-thirds really) was bustling. There was the smell of spirit gum and Max Factor and just plain men. Several guys were getting dressed or un-, and Bruce was cussing Bloody-something because he'd just burnt his fingers unwinding from the neck of a hot electric bulb some crepe hair he'd wound there to dry after wetting and stretching it to turn it from crinkly to straight for his Banquo beard. Bruce is always getting to the theater late and trying shortcuts.

But I had eyes only for Sid. So help me, as soon as I saw him they bugged again. Greta, I told myself, you're going to have to send Martin out to the drugstore for some anti-bug powder. "For the roaches, boy?" "No, for the eyes."

Sid was made up and had his long mustaches and elf-locked Macbeth wig on — and his corset too. I could tell by the way his waist was sucked in before he saw me. But instead of dark kilts and that bronze-studded sweat-stained leather battle harness that lets him show off his beefy shoulders and the top half of his heavily furred chest — and which really does look great on Macbeth in the first act when he comes in straight from battle — but instead of that he was wearing, so help me, red tights cross-gartered with strips of gold-blue tinsel-cloth, a green doublet gold-trimmed and to top it a ruff, and he was trying to fit onto his front a bright silvered cuirass that would have looked just dandy maybe on one of the Pope's Swiss Guards.

I thought, Siddy, Willy S. ought to reach out of his portrait there and bop you one on the koko for contemplating such a crazy-quilt desecration of just about his greatest and certainly his most atmospheric play.

Just then he noticed me and hissed accusingly, "There thou art, slothy minx! Spring to and help stuff me into this monstrous chest-kettle."

"Siddy, what *is* all this?" I demanded as my hands automatically obeyed. "Are you going to play *Macbeth* for laughs, except maybe leaving the Porter a serious character? You think you're Red Skelton?"

"What monstrous brabble is this, you mad bitch?" he retorted, grunting as I bear-hugged his waist, shouldering the cuirass to squeeze it home.

"The clown costumes on all you men," I told him, for now I'd noticed that the others were in rainbow hues, Bruce a real eye-buster in yellow tights and violet doublet as he furiously bushed out and clipped crosswise sections of beard and slapped them on his chin gleaming brown with spirit gum. "I haven't seen any eight-inch polka-dots yet but I'm sure I will."

Suddenly a big grin split Siddy's face and he laughed out loud at me, though the laugh changed to a gasp as I strapped in the cuirass three notches too tight. When we'd got that adjusted he said, "I' faith thou slayest me, pretty witling. Did I not tell you this production is an experiment, a novelty? We shall but show *Macbeth* as it might have been costumed at the court of King James. In the clothes of the day, but gaudier, as was then the stage fashion. Hold, dove, I've somewhat for thee." He fumbled his grouch bag from under his doublet and dipped finger and thumb in it, and put in my palm a silver model of the Empire State Building, charm bracelet size, and one of the new Kennedy dimes.

As I squeezed those two and gloated my eyes on them, feeling securer and happier and friendlier for them though I didn't at the moment want to, I thought, *Well, Siddy's right about that, at least I've read they used to costume the plays that way, though I don't see how Shakespeare stood it. But it was dirty of them all not to tell me beforehand.*

But that's the way it is. Sometimes I'm the butt as well as the pet of the dressing room, and considering all the breaks I get I shouldn't mind. I smiled at Sid and went on tiptoes and necked out my head and kissed him on a powdery cheek just above an aromatic mustache. Then I wiped the smile off my face and said, "Okay, Siddy, play Macbeth as Little Lord Fauntleroy or Baby Snooks if you want to. I'll never squeak again. But the Elizabeth prologue's still an anachronism. And — this is the thing I came to tell you, Siddy — Miss Nefer's not getting ready for any measly prologue. She's set to play Queen Elizabeth all night and tomorrow morning too. Whatever you think, she doesn't know we're doing *Macbeth*. But who'll do Lady Mack if she doesn't? And Martin's not dressing for Malcolm, but for the Son of the Last of the Mohicans, I'd say. What's more —"

You know, something I said must have annoyed Sid, for he changed his mood again in a flash. "Shut your jaw, you crook brained cat, and begone!" he snarled at me. "Here's curtain time close upon us, and you come like a wittol scattering your mad questions like the crazed Ophelia her flowers. Begone, I say!"

"Yessir," I whipped out softly. I skittered off toward the door to the stage, because that was the easiest direction. I figured I could do with a breath of less grease-painty air. Then, "Oh, Greta," I heard Martin call nicely.

He'd changed his levis for black tights, and was stepping into and pulling up around him a very familiar dress, dark green and embroidered with silver and stage-rubies. He'd safety-pinned a folded towel around his chest — to make a bosom of sorts, I realized.

He armed into the sleeves and turned his back to me. "Hook me up, would you?" he entreated.

Then it hit me. They had no actresses in Shakespeare's day, they used boys. And the dark green dress was so familiar to me because —

"Martin," I said, halfway up the hooks and working fast — Miss Nefer's costume fitted him fine. "You're going to play —?"

"Lady Macbeth, yes," he finished for me. "Wish me courage, will you Greta? Nobody else seems to think I need it."

I punched him half-heartedly in the rear. Then, as I fastened the last hooks, my eyes topped his shoulder and I looked at our faces side by side in the mirror of his dressing table. His, in spite of the female edging and him being at least eight years younger than me, I think, looked wise, poised, infinitely resourceful with power in reserve, very very real, while mine looked like that of a bewildered and characterless child ghost about to scatter into air — and the edges of my charcoal sweater and skirt, contrasting with his strong colors, didn't dispel that last illusion.

"Oh, by the way, Greta," he said, "I picked up a copy of *The Village Times* for you. There's a thumbnail review of our *Measure for Measure*, though it mentions no names, darn it. It's around here somewhere...."

But I was already hurrying on. Oh, it was logical enough to have Martin playing Mrs. Macbeth in a production styled to Shakespeare's own times (though pedantically over-authentic, I'd have thought) and it really did answer all my questions, even why Miss Nefer could sink herself wholly in Elizabeth tonight if she wanted to. But it meant that I must be missing so much of what was going on right around me, in spite of spending 24 hours a day in the dressing room, or at most in the small adjoining john or in the wings of the stage just outside the dressing room door, that it scared me. Siddy telling everybody, "*Macbeth* tonight in Elizabethan costume, boys and girls," sure, that I could have missed — though you'd have thought he'd have asked my help on the costumes.

But Martin getting up in Mrs. Mack. Why, someone must have held the part on him twenty-eight times, cueing him, while he got the lines. And there must have been at least a couple of run-through rehearsals to make sure he had all the business and stage movements down pat, and Sid and Martin would have been doing their big scenes every backstage minute they could spare with Sid yelling, "Witling! Think'st *that's* a wifely buss?" and Martin would have been droning his lines last time he scrubbed and mopped. . . .

Greta, they're hiding things from you, I told myself.

Maybe there was a 25th hour nobody had told me about yet when they did all the things they didn't tell me about.

Maybe they were things they didn't dare tell me because of my top-storey weakness.

I felt a cold draft and shivered and I realized I was at the door to the stage.

I should explain that our stage is rather an unusual one, in that it can face two ways, with the drops and set pieces and lighting all capable of being switched around completely. To your left, as you look out the dressing-room door, is an open-air theater, or rather an open-air place for the audience — a large upward-sloping glade walled by thick tall trees and with benches for over two thousand people. On that side the stage kind of merges into the grass and can be made to look part of it by a green groundcloth.

To your right is a big roofed auditorium with the same number of seats.

The whole thing grew out of the free summer Shakespeare performances in Central Park that they started back in the 1950's.

The Janus-stage idea is that in nice weather you can have the audience outdoors, but if it rains or there's a cold snap, or if you want to play all winter without a single break, as we've been doing, then you can put your audience in the auditorium. In that case, a big accordion-pleated wall shuts off the out of doors and keeps the wind from blowing your backdrop, which is on that side, of course, when the auditorium's in use.

Tonight the stage was set up to face the outdoors, although that draft felt mighty chilly.

I hesitated, as I always do at the door to the stage — though it wasn't the actual stage lying just ahead of me, but only backstage, the wings. You see, I always have to fight the feeling that if I go out the dressing room door, go out just eight steps, the world will change while I'm out there and I'll never be able to get back. It won't be New York City any more, but Chicago or Mars or Algiers or Atlanta, Georgia, or Atlantis or Hell and I'll never be able to get back to that lovely warm womb with all the jolly boys and girls and all the costumes smelling like autumn leaves.

Or, especially when there's a cold breeze blowing, I'm afraid that *I'll* change, that I'll grow wrinkled and old in eight footsteps, or shrink down to the witless blob of a baby, or forget altogether who I am —

— or, it occurred to me for the first time now, *remember* who I am. Which might be even worse.

Maybe that's what I'm afraid of.

I took a step back. I noticed something new just beside the door: a high-legged, short-keyboard piano. Then I saw that the legs were those of a table. The piano was just a box with yellowed keys. Spinet? Harpsichord?

"Five minutes, everybody," Martin quietly called out behind me.

I took hold of myself. Greta, I told myself — also for the first time, you know that some day you're really going to have to face this thing, and not just for a quick dip out and back either. Better get in some practice.

I stepped through the door.

Beau and Doc were already out there, made up and in costume for Ross and King Duncan. They were discreetly peering past the wings at the gathering audience. Or at the place where the audience ought to be gathering, at any rate — sometimes the movies and girlie shows and brainheavy beatnik bruhahas outdraw us altogether. Their costumes were the same kooky colorful ones as the others'. Doc had a mock-ermine robe and a huge gilt papier-mache crown. Beau was carrying a ragged black robe and hood over his left arm — he doubles the First Witch.

As I came up behind them, making no noise in my black sneakers, I heard Beau say, "I see some rude fellows from the City approaching. I was hoping we wouldn't get any of those. How should they scent us out?"

Brother, I thought, where do you expect them to come from if not the City? Central Park is bounded on three sides by Manhattan Island and on the fourth by the Eighth Avenue Subway. And Brooklyn and Bronx boys have got pretty sharp scenters. And what's it get you insulting the woiking and non-woiking people of the woild's greatest metropolis? Be grateful for any audience you get, boy.

But I suppose Beau Lassiter considers anybody from north of Vicksburg a "rude fellow" and is always waiting for the day when the entire audience will arrive in carriage and democrat wagons.

Doc replied, holding down his white beard and heavy on the mongrel Russo-German accent he miraculously manages to suppress on stage except when "Vot does it matter? Ve don't convinze zem, ve don't convinze nobody. *Nichevo.*"

Maybe, I thought, Doc shares my doubts about making Macbeth plausible in rainbow pants.

Still unobserved by them, I looked between their shoulders and got the first of my shocks.

It wasn't night at all, but afternoon. A dark cold lowering afternoon, admittedly. But afternoon all the same.

Sure, between shows I sometimes forget whether it's day or night, living inside like I do. But getting matinees and evening performances mixed is something else again.

It also seemed to me, although Beau was leaning in now and I couldn't see so well, that the glade was smaller than it should be, the trees closer to us and more irregular, and I couldn't see the benches. That was Shock Two.

Beau said anxiously, glancing at his wrist, "I wonder what's holding up the Queen?"

Although I was busy keeping up nerve-pressure against the shocks, I managed to think. So he knows about Siddy's stupid Queen Elizabeth prologue too. But of course he would. It's only me they keep in the dark. If he's so smart he ought to remember that Miss Nefer is always the last person on stage, even when she opens the play.

And then I thought I heard, through the trees, the distant drumming of horses' hoofs and the sound of a horn.

Now they do have horseback riding in Central Park and you can hear auto horns there, but the hoofbeats don't drum that wild way. And there aren't so many riding together. And no auto horn I ever heard gave out with that sweet yet imperious *ta-ta-ta-TA*.

I must have squeaked or something, because Beau and Doc turned around quickly, blocking my view, their expressions half angry, half anxious.

I turned too and ran for the dressing room, for I could feel one of my mind-wavery fits coming on. At the last second it had seemed to me that the scenery was getting skimpier, hardly more than thin trees and bushes itself, and underfoot feeling more like ground than a ground cloth, and overhead not theater roof but gray sky. *Shock Three and you're out, Greta*, my umpire was calling.

I made it through the dressing room door and nothing there was wavering or dissolving, praised be Pan. Just Martin standing with his back to me, alert, alive, poised like a cat inside that green dress, the prompt book in his right hand with a finger in it, and from his left hand long black tatters swinging — telling me he'd still be doubling Second Witch. And he was hissing, "Places, please, everybody. On stage!"

With a sweep of silver and ash-colored plush, Miss Nefer came past him, for once leading the last-minute hurry to the stage. She had on the dark red wig now. For me that crowned her characterization. It made me remember her saying, "My brain burns." I ducked aside as if she were majesty incarnate.

And then she didn't break her own precedent. She stopped at the new thing beside the door and poised her long white skinny fingers over the yellowed keys, and suddenly I remembered what it was called: a virginals.

She stared down at it fiercely, evilly, like a witch planning an enchantment. Her face got the secret fiendish look that, I told myself, the real Elizabeth would have had ordering the deaths of Ballard and Babington, or plotting with Drake (for all they say she didn't) one of his raids, that long long forefinger tracing crooked courses through a crabbedly drawn map of the Indies and she smiling at the dots of cities that would burn.

Then all her eight fingers came flickering down and the strings inside the virginals began to twang and hum with a high-pitched rendering of Grieg's "In the Hall of the Mountain King."

Then as Sid and Bruce and Martin rushed past me, along with a black swooping that was Maud already robed and hooded for Third Witch, I beat it for my sleeping closet like Peer Gynt himself dashing across the mountainside away from the cave of the Troll King, who only wanted to make tiny slits in his eyeballs so that forever afterwards he'd see reality just a little differently. And as I ran, the master-anachronism of that menacing mad march music was shrilling in my ears.

III

Sound a dumbe shew. Enter the three fatall sisters, with a
rocke, a threed, and a pair of sheeres.
— Old Play

My sleeping closet is just a cot at the back end of the girls' third of the dressing room, with a three-panel screen to make it private.

When I sleep I hang my outside clothes on the screen, which is pasted and thumbtacked all over with the New York City stuff that gives me security: theater programs and restaurant menus, clippings from the *Times* and the *Mirror*, a torn-out picture of the United Nations building with a hundred tiny gay paper flags pasted around it, and hanging in an old hairnet a home-run baseball autographed by Willy Mays. Things like that.

Right now I was jumping my eyes over that stuff, asking it to keep me located and make me safe, as I lay on my cot in my clothes with my knees drawn up and my fingers over my ears so the louder lines from the play wouldn't be able to come nosing back around the trunks and tables and bright-lit mirrors and find me. Generally I like to listen to them, even if they're sort of sepulchral and drained of overtones by their crooked trip. But they're always tense-making. And tonight (I mean this afternoon) — no!

It's funny I should find security in mementos of a city I daren't go out into — no, not even for a stroll through Central Park, though I know it from the Pond to Harlem Meerth — e Met Museum, the Menagerie, the Ramble, the Great Lawn, Cleopatra's Needle and all the rest. But that's the way it is. Maybe I'm like Jonah in the whale, reluctant to go outside because the whale's a terrible monster that's awful scary to look in the face and might really damage you gulping you a second time, yet reassured to know you're living in the stomach of that particular monster and not a seventeen tentacled one from the fifth planet of Aldebaran.

It's really true, you see, about me actually living in the dressing room. The boys bring me meals: coffee in cardboard cylinders and doughnuts in little brown grease-spotted paper sacks and malts and hamburgers and apples and little pizzas, and Maud brings me raw vegetables — carrots and parsnips and little onions and such, and watches to make sure I exercise my molars grinding them and get my vitamins. I take spit-baths in the little john. Architects don't seem to think actors ever take baths, even when they've browned themselves all over playing Pindarus the Parthian in *Julius Caesar*. And all my shut-eye is caught on this little cot in the twilight of my NYC screen.

You'd think I'd be terrified being alone in the dressing room during the wee and morning hours, let alone trying to sleep then, but that isn't the way it works out. For one thing, there's apt to be someone sleeping in too. Maudie especially. And it's my favorite time too for costume-mending and reading the *Variorum* and other books, and for just plain way-out dreaming. You see, the dressing room is the one place I really do feel safe. Whatever is out there in New York that terrorizes me, I'm pretty confident that it can never get in here.

Besides that, there's a great big bolt on the inside of the dressing room door that I throw whenever I'm all alone after the show. Next day they buzz for me to open it.

It worried me a bit at first and I had asked Sid, "But what if I'm so deep asleep I don't hear and you have to get in fast?" and he had replied, "Sweetling, a word in your ear: our own Beauregard Lassiter is the prettiest picklock unjailed since Jimmy Valentine and Jimmy Dale. I'll not ask where he learned his trade, but 'tis sober truth, upon my honor."

And Beau had confirmed this with a courtly bow, murmuring, "At your service, Miss Greta."

"How do you jigger a big iron bolt through a three-inch door that fits like Maudie's tights?" I wanted to know.

"He carries lodestones of great power and divers subtle tools," Sid had explained for him.

I don't know how they work it so that some Traverse-Three cop or park official doesn't find out about me and raise a stink. Maybe Sid just throws a little more of the temperament he uses to keep most outsiders out of the dressing-room. We sure don't get any janitors or scrubwomen, as Martin and I know only too well. More likely he squares someone. I do get the impression all the company's gone a little way out on a limb letting me stay here — that the directors of our theater wouldn't like it if they found out about me.

In fact, the actors are all so good about helping me and putting up with my antics (though they have their own, Danu digs!) that I sometimes think I must be related to one of them — a distant cousin or sister-in-law (or wife, my God!), because I've checked our faces side by side in the mirrors often enough and I can't find any striking family resemblances. Or maybe I was even an actress in the company. The least important one. Playing the tiniest roles like Lucius in *Caesar* and Bianca in *Othello* and one of the little princes in *Dick the Three Eyes* and Fleance and the Gentlewoman in

Macbeth, though me doing even that much acting strikes me to laugh.

But whatever I am in that direction — if I'm anything — not one of the actors has told me a word about it or dropped the least hint. Not even when I beg them to tell me or try to trick them into it, presumably because it might revive the shock that gave me agoraphobia and amnesia in the first place, and maybe this time knock out my entire mind or at least smash the new mouse-in-a-hole consciousness I've made for myself.

I guess they must have got by themselves a year ago and talked me over and decided my best chance for cure or for just bumping along half happily was staying in the dressing room rather than being sent home (funny, could I have another?) or to a mental hospital. And then they must have been cocky enough about their amateur psychiatry and interested enough in me (the White Horse knows why) to go ahead with a program almost any psychiatrist would be bound to yike at.

I got so worried about the set up once and about the risks they might be running that, gritting down my dread of the idea, I said to Sid, "Siddy, shouldn't I see a doctor?"

He looked at me solemnly for a couple of seconds and then said, "Sure, why not? Go talk to Doc right now," tipping a thumb toward Doc Pyeskov, who was just sneaking back into the bottom of his makeup box what looked like a half pint from the flask I got. I did, incidentally. Doc explained to me Kraepelin's classification of the psychoses, muttering, as he absentmindedly fondled my wrist, that in a year or two he'd be a good illustration of Korsakov's Syndrome.

They've all been pretty darn good to me in their kooky ways, the actors have. Not one of them has tried to take advantage of my situation to extort anything out of me, beyond asking me to sew on a button or polish some boots or at worst clean the wash bowl. Not one of the boys has made a pass I didn't at least seem to invite. And when my crush on Sid was at its worst he shouldered me off by getting polite —

something he only is to strangers. On the rebound I hit Beau, who treated me like a real Southern gentleman.

All this for a stupid little waif, whom anyone but a gang of sentimental actors would have sent to Bellevue without a second thought or feeling. For, to get disgustingly realistic, my most plausible theory of me is that I'm a stage-struck girl from Iowa who saw her twenties slipping away and her sanity too, and made the dash to Greenwich Village, and went so ape on Shakespeare after seeing her first performance in Central Park that she kept going back there night after night (Christopher Street, Penn Station, Times Square, Columbus Circle — see?) and hung around the stage door, so mousy but open-mouthed that the actors made a pet of her.

And then something very nasty happened to her, either down at the Village or in a dark corner of the Park. Something so nasty that it blew the top of her head right off. And she ran to the only people and place where she felt she could ever again feel safe. And she showed them the top of her head with its singed hair and its jagged ring of skull and they took pity.

My least plausible theory of me, but the one I like the most, is that I was born in the dressing room, cradled in the top of a flat theatrical trunk with my ears full of Shakespeare's lines before I ever said "Mama," let alone lamped a TV; hush-walked when I cried by whoever was off stage, old props my first toys, trying to eat crepe hair my first indiscretion, sticks of grease-paint my first crayons. You know, I really wouldn't be bothered by crazy fears about New York changing and the dressing room shifting around in space and time, if I could be sure I'd always be able to stay in it and that the same sweet guys and gals would always be with me and that the shows would always go on.

This show was sure going on, it suddenly hit me, for I'd let my fingers slip off my ears as I sentimentalized and wish-dreamed and I heard, muted by the length and stuff of the dressing room, the slow beat of a drum and then a drum note in Maudie's voice taking up that beat as she warned the other two witches, "A drum, a drum! Macbeth doth come."

Why, I'd not only missed Sid's history-making-and-breaking Queen Elizabeth prologue (kicking myself that I had, now it was over), I'd also missed the short witch scene with its famous "Fair is foul and foul is fair," the Bloody Sergeant scene where Duncan hears about Macbeth's victory, and we were well into the second witch scene, the one on the blasted heath where Macbeth gets it predicted to him he'll be king after Duncan and is tempted to speculate about hurrying up the process.

I sat up. I did hesitate a minute then, my fingers going back toward my ears, because *Macbeth* is specially tense-making and when I've had one of my mind-wavery fits I feel weak for a while and things are blurry and uncertain. Maybe I'd better take a couple of the barbiturate sleeping pills Maudie manages to get for me and — but *No, Greta,* I told myself, *you want to watch this show, you want to see how they do in those crazy costumes. You especially want to see how Martin makes out. He'd never forgive you if you didn't.*

So I walked to the other end of the empty dressing room, moving quite slowly and touching the edges here and there, the words of the play getting louder all the time. By the time I got to the door Bruce-Banquo was saying to the witches, "If you can look into the seeds of time, And say which grain will grow and which will not,"— those lines that stir anyone's imagination with their veiled vision of the universe.

The overall lighting was a little dim (afternoon fading already? — a *late* matinee?) and the stage lights flickery and the scenery still a little spectral-flimsy. Oh, my mind-wavery fits can be lulus! But I concentrated on the actors, watching them through the entrance-gaps in the wings. They were solid enough.

Giving a solid performance, too, as I decided after watching that scene through and the one after it where Duncan congratulates Macbeth, with never a pause between the two scenes in true Elizabethan style. Nobody was laughing at the colorful costumes. After a while I began to accept them myself.

Oh, it was a different *Macbeth* than our company usually does. Louder and faster, with shorter pauses between speeches, the blank verse at times approaching a chant. But it had a lot of real guts and everybody was just throwing themselves into it, Sid especially.

The first Lady Macbeth scene came. Without exactly realizing it I moved forward to where I'd been when I got my three shocks. Martin is so intent on his career and making good that he has me the same way about it.

The Thaness started off, as she always does, toward the opposite side of the stage and facing a little away from me. Then she moved a step and looked down at the stage-parchment letter in her hands and began to read it, though there was nothing on it but scribble, and my heart sank because the voice I heard was Miss Nefer's. I thought (and almost said out loud) *Oh, dammit, he funked out, or Sid decided at the last minute he couldn't trust him with the part. Whoever got Miss Nefer out of the ice cream cone in time?*

Then she swung around and I saw that no, my God, it *was* Martin, no mistaking. He'd been using her voice. When a person first does a part, especially getting up in it without much rehearsing, he's bound to copy the actor he's been hearing doing it. And as I listened on, I realized it was fundamentally Martin's own voice pitched a trifle high, only some of the intonations and rhythms were Miss Nefer's. He was showing a lot of feeling and intensity too and real Martin-type poise. *You're off to a great start, kid*, I cheered inwardly. *Keep it up!*

Just then I looked toward the audience. Once again I almost squeaked out loud. For out there, close to the stage, in the very middle of the reserve section, was a carpet spread out. And sitting in the middle of it on some sort of little chair, with what looked like two charcoal braziers smoking to either side of her, was Miss Nefer with a string of extras in Elizabethan hats with cloaks pulled around them.

For a second it really threw me because it reminded me of the things I'd seen or thought I'd seen the couple of times I'd sneaked a peek through the curtain-hole at the audience in the indoor auditorium.

It hardly threw me for more than a second, though, because I remembered that the characters who speak Shakespeare's prologues often stay on stage and sometimes kind of join the audience and even comment on the play from time to time — Christopher Sly and attendant lords in *The Shrew*, for one. Sid had just copied and in his usual style laid it on thick.

Well, bully for you, Siddy, I thought, I'm sure the witless New York groundlings will be thrilled to their cold little toes knowing they're sitting in the same audience as Good Queen Liz and attendant courtiers. And as for you, Miss Nefer, I added a shade invidiously, you just keep on sitting cold in Central Park, warmed by dry-ice smoke from braziers, and keep your mouth shut and everything'll be fine. I'm sincerely glad you'll be able to be Queen Elizabeth all night long. Just so long as you don't try to steal the scene from Martin and the rest of the cast, and the real play.

I suppose that camp chair will get a little uncomfortable by the time the Fifth Act comes tramping along to that drumbeat, but I'm sure you're so much in character you'll never feel it.

One thing though: just don't scare me again pretending to work witchcraft — with a virginals or any other way.

Okay?

Swell.

Me, now, I'm going to watch the play.

IV

. . . to dream of new dimensions,
Cheating checkmate
by painting the king's robe
So that he slides like a queen;
    — Graves

I swung back to the play just at the moment Lady Mack solil-
oquizes, "Come to my woman's breasts. And take my milk for
gall, you murdering ministers." Although I knew it was just
folded towel Martin was touching with his fingertips as he
lifted them to the top half of his green bodice, I got carried
away, he made it so real. I decided boys can play girls better
than people think. Maybe they should do it a little more often,
and girls play boys too.

Then Sid-Macbeth came back to his wife from the wars,
looking triumphant but scared because the murder-idea's
started to smoulder in him, and she got busy fanning the
blaze like any other good little *hausfrau* intent on her hus-
band rising in the company and knowing that she's the power
behind him and that when there are promotions someone's
always got to get the axe. Sid and Martin made this charming
little domestic scene so natural yet gutsy too that I wanted to
shout hooray. Even Sid clutching Martin to that ridiculous
pot-chested cuirass didn't have one note of horseplay in it.
Their bodies spoke. It was the McCoy.

After that, the play began to get real good, the fast tempo
and exaggerated facial expressions actually helping it. By the
time the Dagger Scene came along I was digging my fingernails into my sweaty palms. Which was a good thing — my
eating up the play, I mean — because it kept me from looking
at the audience again, even taking a fast peek. As you've gath-
ered, audiences bug me. All those people out there in the
shadows, watching the actors in the light, all those silent voy-
eurs as Bruce calls them. Why, they might be anything. And

sometimes (to my mind-wavery sorrow) I think they are. Maybe crouching in the dark out there, hiding among the others, is the one who did the nasty thing to me that tore off the top of my head.

Anyhow, if I so much as glance at the audience, I begin to get ideas about it — and sometimes even if I don't, as just at this moment I thought I heard horses restlessly pawing hard ground and one whinny, though that was shut off fast. *Krishna kressed us!* I thought, *Skiddy can't have hired horses for Nefer-Elizabeth much as he's a circus man at heart. We don't have that kind of money. Besides —*

But just then Sid-Macbeth gasped as if he were sucking in a bucket of air. He'd shed the cuirass, fortunately. He said, "Is this a dagger which I see before me, the handle toward my hand?" and the play hooked me again, and I had no time to think about or listen for anything else. Most of the offstage actors were on the other side of the stage, as that's where they make their exits and entrances at this point in the Second Act. I stood alone in the wings, watching the play like a bug, frightened only of the horrors Shakespeare had in mind when he wrote it.

Yes, the play was going great. The Dagger Scene was terrific where Duncan gets murdered offstage, and so was the part afterwards where hysteria mounts as the crime's discovered.

But just at this point I began to catch notes I didn't like. Twice someone was late on entrance and came on as if shot from a cannon. And three times at least Sid had to throw someone a line when they blew up — in the clutches Sid's better than any prompt book. It began to look as if the play were getting out of control, maybe because the new tempo was so hot.

But they got through the Murder Scene okay. As they came trooping off, yelling "Well contented," most of them on my side for a change, I went for Sid with a towel. He always sweats like a pig in the Murder Scene. I mopped his neck and shoved the towel up under his doublet to catch the dripping armpits.

Meanwhile he was fumbling around on a narrow table where they lay props and costumes for quick changes. Suddenly he dug his fingers into my shoulder, enough to catch my attention at this point, meaning I'd show bruises tomorrow, and yelled at me under his breath, "And you love me, our crows and robes. Presto!"

I was off like a flash to the costumery. There were Mr. and Mrs. Mack's king-and-queen robes and stuff hanging and sitting just where I knew they'd have to be.

I snatched them up, thinking, Boy, they made a mistake when they didn't tell about this special performance, and I started back like Flash Two.

As I shot out the dressing room door the theater was very quiet. There's a short low-pitched scene on stage then, to give the audience a breather. I heard Miss Nefer say loudly (it had to be loud to get to me from even the front of the audience): "'Tis a good bloody play, Eyes," and some voice I didn't recognize reply a bit grudgingly, "There's meat in it and some poetry too, though rough-wrought." She went on, still as loudly as if she owned the theater, "'Twill make Master Kyd bite his nails with jealousy — ha, ha!"

Ha-ha yourself, you scene-stealing witch, I thought, as I helped Sid and then Martin on with their royal outer duds. But at the same time I knew Sid must have written those lines himself to go along with his prologue. They had the unmistakable rough-wrought Lessingham touch. Did he really expect the audience to make anything of that reference to Shakespeare's predecessor Thomas Kyd of *The Spanish Tragedy* and the lost *Hamlet*? And if they knew enough to spot that, wouldn't they be bound to realize the whole Elizabeth-Macbeth tie-up was anachronistic? But when Sid gets an inspiration he can be very bull-headed.

Just then, while Bruce-Banquo was speaking his broody low soliloquy on stage, Miss Nefer cut in again loudly with,

"Aye, Eyes, a good bloody play. Yet somehow, methinks — I know not how — I've heard it before." Whereupon Sid grabbed Martin by the wrist and hissed, "Did'st hear? Oh, I like not that," and I thought, *Oh-ho, so now she's beginning to ad-lib.*

Well, right away they all went on stage with a flourish, Sid and Martin crowned and hand in hand. The play got going strong again. But there were still those edge-of-control undercurrents and I began to be more uneasy than caught up, and I had to stare consciously at the actors to keep off a wavery-fit.

Other things began to bother me too, such as all the doubling.

Macbeth's a great play for doubling. For instance, anyone except Macbeth or Banquo can double one of the Three Witches — or one of the Three Murderers for that matter. Normally we double at least one or two of the Witches and Murderers, but this performance there'd been more multiple-parting than I'd ever seen. Doc had whipped off his Duncan beard and thrown on a brown smock and hood to play the Porter with his normal bottle-roughened accents. Well, a drunk impersonating a drunk, pretty appropriate. But Bruce was doing the next-door-to-impossible double of Banquo and Macduff, using a ringing tenor voice for the latter and wearing in the murder scene a helmet with dropped visor to hide his Banquo beard. He'd be able to tear it off, of course, after the Murderers got Banquo and he'd made his brief appearance as a bloodied-up ghost in the Banquet Scene. I asked myself, *My God, has Siddy got all the other actors out in front playing courtiers to Elizabeth-Nefer? Wasting them that way? The whoreson rogue's gone nuts!*

But really it was plain frightening, all that frantic doubling and tripling with its suggestion that the play (and the company too, Freya forfend) was becoming a ricketty patchwork illusion with everybody racing around faster and faster to hide the holes. And the scenery-wavery stuff and the warped Park-sounds were scary too. I was actually shivering by the time Sid got to: "Light thickens; and the crow Makes wing to the rooky wood: Good things of day begin to droop and drowse; Whiles night's black agents to their preys do rouse." Those graveyard lines didn't help my nerves any, of course. Nor did thinking I heard Nefer-Elizabeth say from the audience, rather softly for her this time, "Eyes, I have heard that speech, I know not where. Think you 'tiz stolen?"

Greta, I told myself, you need a miltown before the crow makes wing through your kooky head.

I turned to go and fetch me one from my closet. And stopped dead.

Just behind me, pacing back and forth like an ash-colored tiger in the gloomy wings, looking daggers at the audience every time she turned at that end of her invisible cage, but ignoring me completely, was Miss Nefer in the Elizabeth wig and rig.

Well, I suppose I should have said to myself, Greta, you imagined that last loud whisper from the audience. Miss Nefer's simply unkinked herself, waved a hand to the real audience and come back stage. Maybe Sid just had her out there for the first half of the play. Or maybe she just couldn't stand watching Martin give such a bang-up performance in her part of Lady Mack.

Yes, maybe I should have told myself something like that, but somehow all I could think then — and I thought it with a steady mounting shiver — was, *We got two Elizabeths. This one is our witch Nefer. I know. I dressed her. And I know that devil-look from the virginals. But if this is our Elizabeth, the company Elizabeth, the stage Elizabeth . . . who's the other?*

And because I didn't dare to let myself think of the answer to that question, I dodged around the invisible cage that the ash-colored skirt seemed to ripple against as the Tiger Queen turned and I ran into the dressing room, my only thought to get behind my New York City Screen.

V

Even little things are turning out to be great things and becoming intensely interesting.
Have you ever thought about the properties of numbers?
— The Maiden

Lying on my cot, my eyes crosswise to the printing, I looked from a pink Algonquin menu to a pale green New Amsterdam program, with a tiny doll of Father Knickerbocker dangling between them on a yellow thread. Really they weren't covering up much of anything. A ghostly hole an inch and a half across seemed to char itself in the program. As if my eye were right up against it, I saw in vivid memory what I'd seen the two times I'd dared a peek through the hole in the curtain: a bevy of ladies in masks and Nell Gwyn dresses and men in King Charles knee-breeches and long curled hair, and the second time a bunch of people and creatures just wild: all sorts and colors of clothes, humans with hoofs for feet and antennae springing from their foreheads, furry and feathery things that had more arms than two and in one case that many heads — as if they were dressed up in our *Tempest, Peer Gynt* and *Insect People* costumes and some more besides.

Naturally I'd had mind-wavery fits both times. Afterwards Sid had wagged a finger at me and explained that on those two nights we'd been giving performances for people who'd arranged a costume theater-party and been going to attend a masquerade ball, and 'zounds, when would I learn to guard my half-patched pate?

I don't know, I guess never, I answered now, quick looking at a Giants pennant, a Korvette ad, a map of Central Park, my Willy Mays baseball and a Radio City tour ticket. That was eight items I'd looked at this trip without feeling any inward improvement. They weren't reassuring me at all.

The blue fly came slowly buzzing down over my screen and I asked it, "What are you looking for? A spider?" when what should I hear coming back through the dressing room straight toward my sleeping closet but Miss Nefer's footsteps. No one else walks that way.

She's going to do something to you, Greta, I thought. She's the maniac in the company. She's the one who terrorized you with the boning knife in the shrubbery, or sicked the giant tarantula on you at the dark end of the subway platform, or whatever it was, and the others are covering up for. She's going to smile the devil-smile and weave those white twig-fingers at you, all eight of them. And Birnam Wood'll come to Dunsinane and you'll be burnt at the stake by men in armor or drawn and quartered by eight-legged monkeys that talk or torn apart by wild centaurs or whirled through the roof to the moon without being dressed for it or sent burrowing into the past to stifle in Iowa 1948 or Egypt 4,008 B.C. The screen won't keep her out.

Then a head of hair pushed over the screen. But it was black-bound-with-silver, Brahma bless us, and a moment later Martin was giving me one of his rare smiles.

I said, "Marty, do something for me. Don't ever use Miss Nefer's footsteps again. Her voice, okay, if you have to. But not the footsteps. Don't ask me why, just don't."

Martin came around and sat on the foot of my cot. My legs were already doubled up. He straightened out his blue-and-gold skirt and rested a hand on my black sneakers.

"Feeling a little wonky, Greta?" he asked. "Don't worry about me. Banquo's dead and so's his ghost. We've finished the Banquet Scene. I've got lots of time."

I just looked at him, queerly I guess. Then without lifting my head I asked him, "Martin, tell me the truth. Does the dressing room move around?"

I was talking so low that he hitched a little closer, not touching me anywhere else though.

"The Earth's whipping around the sun at 20 miles a second," he replied, "and the dressing room goes with it."

I shook my head, my cheek scrubbing the pillow, "I

mean . . . shifting," I said. "By itself."

"How?" he asked.

"Well," I told him, "I've had this idea — it's just a sort of fancy, remember — that if you wanted to time-travel and, well, do things, you could hardly pick a more practical machine than a dressing room and sort of stage and half-theater attached, with actors to man it. Actors can fit in anywhere. They're used to learning new parts and wearing strange costumes. Heck, they're even used to traveling a lot. And if an actor's a bit strange nobody thinks anything of it — he's almost expected to be foreign, it's an asset to him."

"And a theater, well, a theater can spring up almost anywhere and nobody ask questions, except the zoning authorities and such and they can always be squared. Theaters come and go. It happens all the time. They're transitory. Yet theaters are crossroads, anonymous meeting places, anybody with a few bucks or sometimes nothing at all can go. And theaters attract important people, the sort of people you might want to do something to. Caesar was stabbed in a theater. Lincoln was shot in one. And. . . ."

My voice trailed off. "A cute idea," he commented.

I reached down to his hand on my shoe and took hold of his middle finger as a baby might.

"Yeah," I said, "But Martin, is it true?"

He asked me gravely, "What do you think?"

I didn't say anything.

"How would you like to work in a company like that?" he asked speculatively.

"I don't really know," I said.

He sat up straighter and his voice got brisk. "Well, all fantasy aside, how'd you like to work in this company?" He asked, lightly slapping my ankle. "On the stage, I mean. Sid thinks you're ready for some of the smaller parts. In fact, he asked me to put it to you. He thinks you never take him seriously."

"Pardon me while I gasp and glow," I said. Then, "Oh

Marty, I can't really imagine myself doing the tiniest part."

"Me neither, eight months ago," he said. "Now, look. Lady Macbeth."

"But Marty," I said, reaching for his finger again, "you haven't answered my question. About whether it's true."

"Oh that!" he said with a laugh, switching his hand to the other side. "Ask me something else."

"Okay," I said, "why am I bugged on the number eight? Because I'm permanently behind a private 8-ball?"

"Eight's a number with many properties," he said, suddenly as intently serious as he usually is. "The corners of a cube."

"You mean I'm a square?" I said. "Or just a brick? You know, 'She's a brick.'"

"But eight's most curious property," he continued with a frown, "is that lying on its side it signifies infinity. So eight erect is really —" and suddenly his made-up, naturally solemn face got a great glow of inspiration and devotion — "Infinity Arisen!"

Well, I don't know. You meet quite a few people in the theater who are bats on numerology, they use it to pick stage-names. But I'd never have guessed it of Martin. He always struck me as the skeptical, cynical type.

"I had another idea about eight," I said hesitatingly. "Spiders. That 8-legged asterisk on Miss Nefer's forehead —" I suppressed a shudder.

"You don't like her, do you?" he stated.

"I'm afraid of her," I said.

"You shouldn't be. She's a very great woman and tonight she's playing an infinitely more difficult part than I am. No, Greta," he went on as I started to protest, "believe me, you don't understand anything about it at this moment. Just as you don't understand about spiders, fearing them. They're the first to climb the rigging and to climb ashore too. They're the web-weavers, the line-throwers, the connectors, Siva and Kali united in love. They're the double mandala, the beginning and the end, infinity mustered and on the march —"

"They're also on my New York screen!" I squeaked, shrinking back across the cot a little and pointing at a tiny glinting silver-and-black thing mounting below my Willy-ball.

Martin gently caught its line on his finger and lifted it very close to his face. "Eight eyes too," he told me. Then, "Poor little god," he said and put it back.

"Marty? Marty?" Sid's desperate stage-whisper rasped the length of the dressing room.

Martin stood up. "Yes, Sid?"

Sid's voice stayed a whisper but went from desperate to ferocious. "You villainous elf-skin! Know you not the Cauldron Scene's been playing a hundred heartbeats? 'Tis 'most my entrance and we still mustering only two witches out of three! Oh, you nott-pated starveling!"

Before Sid had got much more than half of that out, Martin had slipped around the screen, raced the length of the dressing room, and I'd heard a lusty thwack as he went out the door. I couldn't help grinning, though with Martin racked by anxieties and reliefs over his first time as Lady Mack, it was easy to understand it slipping his mind that he was still doubling Second Witch.

VI

I will vault credit
and affect high pleasures
Beyond death.
  — Ferdinand

I sat down where Martin had been, first pushing the screen far enough to the side for me to see the length of the dressing room and notice anyone coming through the door and any blurs moving behind the thin white curtain shutting off the boys' two-thirds.

I'd been going to think. But instead I just sat there, experiencing my body and the room around it, steadying myself or maybe readying myself. I couldn't tell which, but it was nothing to think about, only to feel. My heartbeat became a very faint, slow, solid throb. My spine straightened.

No one came in or went out. Distantly I heard Macbeth and the witches and the apparitions talk.

Once I looked at the New York Screen, but all the stuff there had grown stale. No protection, no nothing.

I reached down to my suitcase and from where I'd been going to get a miltown I took a dexedrine and popped it in my mouth. Then I started out, beginning to shake.

When I got to the end of the curtain I went around it to Sid's dressing table and asked Shakespeare, "Am I doing the right thing, Pop?" But he didn't answer me out of his portrait. He just looked sneaky-innocent, like he knew a lot but wouldn't tell, and I found myself think of a little silver-framed photo Sid had used to keep there too of a cocky German-looking young actor with "Erich" autographed across it in white ink. At least I supposed he was an actor. He looked a little like Erich von Stroheim, but nicer yet somehow nastier too. The photo had used to upset me, I don't know why. Sid must have noticed it, for one day it was gone.

I thought of the tiny black-and-silver spider crawling across the remembered silver frame, and for some reason it gave me the cold creeps.

Well, this wasn't doing me any good, just making me feel dismal again, so I quickly went out. In the door I had to slip around the actors coming back from the Cauldron Scene and the big bolt nicked my hip.

Outside Maud was peeling off her Third Witch stuff to reveal Lady Macduff beneath. She twitched me a grin.

"How's it going?" I asked.

"Okay, I guess," she shrugged. "What an audience! Noisy as highschool kids."

"How come Sid didn't have a boy do your part?" I asked.

"He goofed, I guess. But I've battened down my bosoms and playing Mrs. Macduff as a boy."

"How does a girl do that in a dress?" I asked.

"She sits stiff and thinks pants," she said, handing me her witch robe. "'Scuse me now. I got to find my children and go get murdered."

I'd moved a few steps nearer the stage when I felt the gentlest tug at my hip. I looked down and saw that a taut black thread from the bottom of my sweater connected me with the dressing room. It must have snagged on the big bolt and unraveled. I moved my body an inch or so, tugging it delicately to see what it felt like and I got the answers: Theseus's clew, a spider's line, an umbilicus.

I reached down close to my side and snapped it with my fingernails. The black thread leaped away. But the dressing room door didn't vanish, or the wings change, or the world end, and I didn't fall down.

After that I just stood there for quite a while, feeling my new freedom and steadiness, letting my body get used to it. I didn't do any thinking. I hardly bothered to study anything around me, though I did notice that there were more bushes and trees than set pieces, and that the flickery lightning was simply torches and that Queen Elizabeth was in (or back in) the audience. Sometimes letting your body get used to something is all you should do, or maybe can do.

And I did smell horse dung.

When the Lady Macduff Scene was over and the Chicken Scene well begun, I went back to the dressing room. Actors call it the Chicken Scene because Macduff weeps in it about "all my pretty chickens and their dam," meaning his kids and wife, being murdered "at one fell swoop" on orders of that chickenyard-raiding "hell-kite" Macbeth.

Inside the dressing room I steered down the boys' side. Doc was putting on an improbable-looking dark makeup for Macbeth's last faithful servant Seyton. He didn't seem as boozy-woozy as usual for Fourth Act, but just the same I stopped to help him get into a chain-mail shirt made of thick cord woven and silvered.

In the third chair beyond, Sid was sitting back with his corset loosened and critically surveying Martin, who'd now changed to a white wool nightgown that clung and draped beautifully, but not particularly enticingly, on him and his folded towel, which had slipped a bit.

From beside Sid's mirror, Shakespeare smiled out of his portrait at them like an intelligent big-headed bug.

Martin stood tall, spread his arms rather like a high priest, and intoned, "*Amici! Romani! Populares!*"

I nudged Doc. "What goes on now?" I whispered.

He turned a bleary eye on them. "I think they are rehearsing *Julius Caesar* in Latin." He shrugged. "It begins the oration of Antony."

"But why?" I asked. Sid does like to put every moment to use when the performance-fire is in people, but this project seemed pretty far afield — hyper-pedantic. Yet at the same time I felt my scalp shivering as if my mind were jumping with speculations just below the surface.

Doc shook his head and shrugged again.

Sid shoved a palm at Martin and roared softly, "'Sdeath, boy, thou'rt not playing a Roman statua but a Roman! Loosen your knees and try again."

Then he saw me. Signing Martin to stop, he called, "Come hither, sweetling." I obeyed quickly. He gave me a fiendish grin and said, "Thou'st heard our proposal from Martin. What sayest thou, wench?"

This time the shiver was in my back. It felt good. I realized I was grinning back at him, and I knew what I'd been getting ready for the last twenty minutes.

"I'm on," I said. "Count me in the company."

Sid jumped up and grabbed me by the shoulders and hair and bussed me on both cheeks. It was a little like being bombed.

"Prodigious!" he cried. "Thou'lt play the Gentlewoman

in the Sleepwalking Scene tonight. Martin, her costume! Now sweet wench, mark me well." His voice grew grave and old. "When was it she last walked?"

The new courage went out of me like water down a chute. "But Siddy, I can't start *tonight*," I protested, half pleading, half outraged.

"Tonight or never! 'Tis an emergency — we're short-handed." Again his voice changed. "When was it she last walked?"

"But Siddy, I don't *know* the part."

"You must. You've heard the play twenty times this year past. When was it she last walked?"

Martin was back and yanking down a blonde wig on my head and shoving my arms into a light gray robe.

"I've never studied *the lines*," I squeaked at Sidney.

"Liar! I've watched your lips move a dozen nights when you watched the scene from the wings. Close your eyes, girl! Martin, unhand her. Close your eyes, girl, empty your mind, and listen, listen only. When was it she last walked?"

In the blackness I heard myself replying to that cue, first in a whisper, then more loudly, then full-throated but grave, "Since his majesty went into the field, I have seen her rise from her bed, throw her nightgown upon her, unlock her closet, take forth —"

"Bravissimo!" Siddy cried and bombed me again. Martin hugged his arm around my shoulders too, then quickly stooped to start hooking up my robe from the bottom.

"But that's only the first lines, Siddy," I protested.

"They're enough!"

"But Siddy, what if I blow up?" I asked.

"Keep your mind empty. You won't. Further, I'll be at your side, doubling the Doctor, to prompt you if you pause."

That ought to take care of two of me, I thought. Then something else struck me. "But Siddy," I quavered, "how do I play the Gentlewoman as a boy?"

"Boy?" he demanded wonderingly. "Play her without fall-

ing down flat on your face and I'll be past measure happy!"
And he smacked me hard on the fanny.

Martin's fingers were darting at the next to the last hook.
I stopped him and shoved my hand down the neck of my
sweater and got hold of the subway token and the chain it was
on and yanked. It burned my neck but the gold links parted. I
started to throw it across the room, but instead I smiled at
Siddy and dropped it in his palm.

"The Sleepwalking Scene!" Maud hissed insistently to us
from the door.

VII

I know death hath ten thousand several doors
For men to take their exits, and 'tis found
They go on such strange geometrical hinges,
You may open them both ways.
— The Duchess

There is this about an actor on stage: he can see the audience
but he can't *look* at them, unless he's a narrator or some sort
of comic. I wasn't the first (Grendel groks!) and only scared
to death of becoming the second as Siddy walked me out of
the wings onto the stage, over the groundcloth that felt so
much like ground, with a sort of interweaving policeman-
grip on my left arm.

Sid was in a dark gray robe looking like some dismal kind
of monk, his head so hooded for the Doctor that you couldn't
see his face at all.

My skull was pulse-buzzing. My throat was squeezed dry.
My heart was pounding. Below that my body was empty,
squirmy, electricity-stung, yet with the feeling of wearing ice
cold iron pants.

I heard as if from two million miles, "When was it she last
walked?" and then an iron bell somewhere tolling the reply —
I guess it had to be my voice coming up through my body

from my iron pants: "Since his majesty went into the field —"
and so on, until Martin had come on stage, stary-eyed, a
white scarf tossed over the back of his long black wig and a
flaring candle two inches thick gripped in his right hand and
dripping wax on his wrist, and started to do Lady Mack's
sleepwalking half-hinted confessions of the murders of
Duncan and Banquo and Lady Macduff.

So here is what I saw then without looking, like a vivid
scene that floats out in front of your mind in a reverie, hov-
ering against a background of dark blur, and sort of flashes on
and off as you think, or in my case act. All the time, remember, with Sid's hand hard on my wrist and me now and
then tolling Shakespearan language out of some lightless
storehouse of memory I'd never known was there to belong to
me.

There was a medium-size glade in a forest. Through the
half-naked black branches shone a dark cold sky, like ashes of
silver, early evening.

The glade had two horns, as it were, narrowing back to
either side and going off through the forest. A chilly breeze
was blowing out of them, almost enough to put out the
candle. Its flame rippled.

Rather far back in the horn to my left, but not very far,
were clumped two dozen or so men in dark cloaks they hud-
dled around themselves. They wore brimmed tallish hats and
pale stuff showing at their necks. Somehow I assumed that
these men must be the "rude fellows from the City" I remembered Beau mentioning a million or so years ago. Although I
couldn't see them very well, and didn't spend much time on
them, there was one of them who had his hat off or excitedly
pushed way back, showing a big pale forehead. Although that
was all the conscious impression I had of his face, he seemed
frighteningly familiar.

In the horn to my right, which was wider, were lined up
about a dozen horses, with grooms holding tight every two of
them, but throwing their heads back now and then as they

strained against the reins, and stamping their front hooves restlessly. Oh, they frightened me, I tell you, that line of two-foot-long glossy-haired faces, writhing back their upper lips from teeth wide as piano keys, every horse of them looking as wild-eyed and evil as Fuseli's steed sticking its head through the drapes in his picture "The Nightmare."

To the center the trees came close to the stage. Just in front of them was Queen Elizabeth sitting on the chair on the spread carpet, just as I'd seen her out there before; only now I could see that the braziers were glowing and redly high-lighting her pale cheeks and dark red hair and the silver in her dress and cloak. She was looking at Martin — Lady Mack — most intently, her mouth grimaced tight, twisting her fingers together.

Standing rather close around her were a half dozen men with fancier hats and ruffs and wide-flaring riding gauntlets.

Then, through the trees and tall leafless bushes just be-hind Elizabeth, I saw an identical Elizabeth-face floating, only this one was smiling a demonic smile. The eyes were open very wide. Now and then the pupils darted rapid glances from side to side.

There was a sharp pain in my left wrist and Sid whisper-snarling at me, "Accustomed action!" out of the corner of his shadowed mouth.

I tolled on obediently, "It is an accustomed action with her, to seem thus washing her hands: I have known her con-tinue in this a quarter of an hour."

Martin had set down the candle, which still flared and guttered, on a little high table so firm its thin legs must have been stabbed into the ground. And he was rubbing his hands together slowly, continually, tormentedly, trying to get rid of Duncan's blood which Mrs. Mack knows in her sleep is still there. And all the while as he did it, the agitation of the seated Elizabeth grew, the eyes flicking from side to side, hands writhing.

He got to the lines, "Here's the smell of blood still: all the perfumes of Arabia will not sweeten this little hand. Oh, oh, oh!"

As he wrung out those soft, tortured sighs, Elizabeth stood up from her chair and took a step forward. The courtiers moved toward her quickly, but not touching her, and she said loudly, "'Tis the blood of Mary Stuart whereof she speaks — the pails of blood that will gush from her chopped neck. Oh, I cannot endure it!" And as she said that last, she suddenly turned about and strode back toward the trees, kicking out her ash-colored skirt. One of the courtiers turned with her and stooped toward her closely, whispering something. But although she paused a moment, all she said was, "Nay, Eyes, stop not the play, but follow me not! Nay, I say leave me, Leicester!" And she walked into the trees, he looking after her.

Then Sid was kicking my ankle and I was reciting something and Martin was taking up his candle again without looking at it saying with a drugged agitation, "To bed; to bed; there's knocking at the gate."

Elizabeth came walking out of the trees again, her head bowed. She couldn't have been in them ten seconds. Leicester hurried toward her, hand anxiously outstretched.

Martin moved offstage, torturedly yet softly wailing, "What's done cannot be undone."

Just then Elizabeth flicked aside Leicester's hand with playful contempt and looked up and she was smiling the devil-smile. A horse whinnied like a trumpeted snicker.

As Sid and I started our last few lines together I intoned mechanically, letting words free-fall from my mind to my tongue. All this time I had been answering Lady Mack in my thoughts, *That's what you think, sister.*

VIII

God cannot effect that anything which is past should not have been.
It is more impossible than rising the dead.
— Summa Theologica

The moment I was out of sight of the audience I broke away from Sid and ran to the dressing room. I flopped down on the first chair I saw, my head and arms trailed over its back, and I almost passed out. It wasn't a mind-wavery fit. Just normal faint.

I couldn't have been there long — well, not very long, though the battle-rattle and alarums of the last scene were echoing tinnily from the stage — when Bruce and Beau and Mark (who was playing Malcolm, Martin's usual main part) came in wearing their last-act stage-armor and carrying between them Queen Elizabeth flaccid as a sack. Martin came after them, stripping off his white wool nightgown so fast that buttons flew. I thought automatically, *I'll have to sew those.*

They laid her down on three chairs set side by side and hurried out. Unpinning the folded towel, which had fallen around his waist, Martin walked over and looked down at her. He yanked off his wig by a braid and tossed it at me.

I let it hit me and fall on the floor. I was looking at that white queenly face, eyes open and staring sightless at the ceiling, mouth open a little too with a thread of foam trailing from the corner, and at that ice-cream-cone bodice that never stirred. The blue fly came buzzing over my head and circled down toward her face.

"Martin," I said with difficulty, "I don't think I'm going to like what we're doing."

He turned on me, his short hair elfed, his fists planted high on his hips at the edge of his black tights, which now were all his clothes.

"You knew!" he said impatiently. "You knew you were

signing up for more than acting when you said, 'Count me in the company.'"

Like a legged sapphire the blue fly walked across her upper lip and stopped by the thread of foam.

"But Martin . . . changing the past . . . dipping back and killing the real queen . . . replacing her with a double —"

His dark brows shot up. "The real — You think this is the real Queen Elizabeth?" He grabbed a bottle of rubbing alcohol from the nearest table, gushed some on a towel stained with grease-paint and, holding the dead head by its red hair (no, wig — the real one wore a wig too) scrubbed the forehead.

The white cosmetic came away, showing sallow skin and on it a faint tattoo in the form of an "S" styled like a yin-yang symbol left a little open.

"Snake!" he hissed. "Destroyer! The arch-enemy, the eternal opponent! God knows how many times people like Queen Elizabeth have been dug out of the past, first by Snakes, then by Spiders, and kidnapped or killed and replaced in the course of our war. This is the first big operation I've been on, Greta. But I know that much."

My head began to ache. I asked, "If she's an enemy double, why didn't she know a performance of Macbeth in her lifetime was an anachronism?"

"Foxholed in the past, only trying to hold a position, they get dulled. They turn half zombie. Even the Snakes. Even our people. Besides, she almost did catch on, twice when she spoke to Leicester."

"Martin," I said dully, "if there've been all these replacements, first by them, then by us, what's happened to the *real* Elizabeth?"

He shrugged. "God knows."

I asked softly, "But does He, Martin? Can He?"

He hugged his shoulders in, as if to contain a shudder. "Look, Greta," he said, "it's the Snakes who are the warpers and destroyers. We're restoring the past. The Spiders are trying to keep things as first created. We only kill when we must."

I shuddered then, for bursting out of my memory came the glittering, knife-flashing, night-shrouded, bloody image of my lover, the Spider soldier-of-change Erich von Hohenwald, dying in the grip of a giant silver spider, or spider-shaped entity large as he, as they rolled in a tangled ball down a flight of rocks in Central Park.

But the memory-burst didn't blow up my mind, as it had done a year ago, no more than snapping the black thread from my sweater had ended the world. I asked Martin, "Is that what the Snakes say?"

"Of course not! They make the same claims we do. But somewhere, Greta, you have to *trust*." He put out the middle finger of his hand.

I didn't take hold of it. He whirled it away, snapping it against his thumb.

"You're still grieving for that carrion there!" he accused me. He jerked down a section of white curtain and whirled it over the stiffening body. "If you must grieve, grieve for Miss Nefer! Exiled, imprisoned, locked forever in the past, her mind pulsing faintly in the black hole of the dead and gone, yearning for Nirvana yet nursing one lone painful patch of consciousness. And only to hold a fort! Only to make sure Mary Stuart is executed, the Armada licked, and that all the other consequences flow on. The Snakes' Elizabeth let Mary live . . . and England die . . . and the Spaniard hold North America to the Great Lakes and New Scandinavia."

Once more he put out his middle finger.

"All right, all right," I said, barely touching it. "You've convinced me."

"Great!" he said. "'Bye for now, Greta. I got to help strike the set."

"That's good," I said. He loped out.

I could hear the skirling sword-clashes of the final fight to the death of the two Macks, Duff and Beth. But I only sat there in the empty dressing room pretending to grieve for a devil-smiling snow tiger locked in a time-cage and for a cute sardonic German killed for insubordination that *I* had reported . . . but really grieving for a girl who for a year had been a rootless child of the theater with a whole company of mothers and fathers, afraid of nothing more than subway bogies and Park and Village monsters.

As I sat there pitying myself beside a shrouded queen, a shadow fell across my knees. I saw stealing through the dressing room a young man in worn dark clothes. He couldn't have been more than twenty-three. He was a frail sort of guy with a weak chin and big forehead and eyes that saw everything. I knew at one he was the one who had seemed familiar to me in the knot of City fellows.

He looked at me and I looked from him to the picture sitting on the reserve makeup box by Siddy's mirror. And I began to tremble.

He looked at it too, of course, as fast as I did. And then he began to tremble too, though it was a finer-grained tremor than mine.

The sword-fight had ended seconds back and now I heard the witches faintly wailing, "Fair is foul, and foul is fair —" Sid has them echo that line offstage at the end to give a feeling of prophecy fulfilled.

Then Sid came pounding up. He's the first finished, since the fight ends offstage so Macduff can carry back a red-necked papier-mache head of him and show it to the audience. Sid stopped dead in the door.

Then the stranger turned around. His shoulders jerked as he saw Sid. He moved toward him just two or three steps at a time, speaking at the same time in breathy little rushes.

Sid stood there and watched him. When the other actors came boiling up behind him, he put his hands on the doorframe to either side so none of them could get past. Their faces peered around him.

And all this while the stranger was saying, "What may this

mean? Can such things be? Are all the seeds of time . . . wetted by some hell-trickle . . . sprouted at once in their granary? Speak . . . speak! You played me a play . . . that I am writing in my secretest heart. Have you disjointed the frame of things . . . to steal my unborn thoughts? Fair is foul indeed. Is all the world a stage? Speak, I say! Are you not my friend Sidney James Lessingham of King's Lynn . . . singed by time's fiery wand . . . sifted over with the ashes of thirty years? Speak, are you not he? Oh, there are more things in heaven and earth . . . aye, and perchance hell too . . . Speak, I charge you!"

And with that he put his hands on Sid's shoulders, half to shake him, I think, but half to keep from falling over. And for the one time I ever saw it, glib old Siddy had nothing to say.

He worked his lips. He opened his mouth twice and twice shut it. Then, with a kind of desperation in his face, he motioned the actors out of the way behind him with one big arm and swung the other around the stranger's narrow shoulders and swept him out of the dressing room, himself following.

The actors came pouring in then, Bruce tossing Macbeth's head to Martin like a football while he tugged off his horned helmet, Mark dumping a stack of shields in the corner, Maudie pausing as she skittered past me to say, "Hi Gret, great you're back," and patting my temple to show what part of me she meant. Beau went straight to Sid's dressing table and set the portrait aside and lifted out Sid's reserve makeup box.

"The lights, Martin!" he called.

Then Sid came back in, slamming and bolting the door behind him and standing for a moment with his back against it, panting.

I rushed to him. Something was boiling up inside me, but before it could get to my brain I opened my mouth and it came out as, "Siddy, you can't fool me, that was no dirty S-or-S. I don't care how much he shakes and purrs, or shakes a spear, or just plain shakes — Siddy, that was Shakespeare!"

"Aye, girl, I think so," he told me, holding my wrists together. "They can't find dolls to double men like that — or such is my main hope." A big sickly grin came on his face. "Oh, gods," he demanded, "with what words do you talk to a man whose speech you've stolen all your life?"

I asked him, "Sid, were we *ever* in Central Park?"

He answered, "Once — twelve months back. A one-night stand. They came for Erich. You flipped."

He swung me aside and moved behind Beau. All the lights went out.

Then I saw, dimly at first, the great dull-gleaming jewel, covered with dials and green-glowing windows, that Beau had lifted from Sid's reserve makeup box. The strongest green glow showed his intent face, still framed by the long glistening locks of the Ross wig, as he kneeled before the thing — Major Maintainer, I remembered it was called.

"When now? Where?" Beau tossed impatiently to Sid over his shoulder.

"The forty-fourth year before our Lord's birth!" Sid answered instantly. "Rome!"

Beau's fingers danced over the dials like a musician's, or a safe-cracker's. The green glow flared and faded flickeringly.

"There's a storm in that vector of the Void."

"Circle it," Sid ordered.

"There are dark mists every way."

"Then pick the likeliest dark path!"

I called through the dark, "Fair is foul, and foul is fair, eh, Siddy?"

"Aye, chick," he answered me. "'Tis all the rule we have!"